HOLY DAYS OF OBLIGATION

HOLY DAYS OF OBLIGATION

SUSAN ZETTELL

NUAGE
EDITIONS

Cover design by Terry Gallagher/Doowah Design.
Cover photograph by Loretta Zettell.
Photo of Susan Zettell by Andy Watt.
Printed and bound in Canada by Marc Veilleux Imprimeur.

Parts of this book have been previously published: "Honeymoon Pants" and "The Mustard Jacket" in *The Canadian Forum,* "The Drawer" in *The New Quarterly,* "Watch" in *The Capilano Review,* and "The Cigarette" in *The University of Windsor Review.*

Acknowledgements
The author wishes to thank: The Canada Council, the Regional Municipality of Ottawa-Carleton and the Ontario Arts Council. The Leighton Artists Colony, Banff Centre for the Arts. Andy Watt. Daniel and John Watt. My family. Andy's family. Frances Itani, Bryan Moon and Jane Urquhart. Laura McLauchlan and Ray Rogers. Susan Brown. Jan Andrews, Mary Brodhead, Trish Cashin, Jennifer Cayley, Heather Evans, Tom Evans, Jan Fraser, Jane Keeler, Helen Levine, Andy Lunney, Barbara Lunney, Lois McVannel, Bea Keleher Raffoul, John Roberts, Faith Schneider, Angela Smith, Bonnie Thompson, Marion Thompson, Pat Whiting. The Virgins From Hell. The University of Ottawa Advanced Writing Workshop. The Ottawa Writing Group.

We acknowledge the support of The Canada Council for the Arts for our publishing program.

Canadian Cataloguing in Publication Data

Zettell, Susan, 1951–
Holy days of obligation

ISBN 0-921833-61-X

I. Title.

PS8599.E88H65 1998 C813'.54 C98-901089-9
PR9199.3.Z48H65 1998

Nuage Editions, P.O. Box 206, RPO Corydon, Winnipeg, Manitoba, R3M 3S7

For Loretta and Jerry Zettell

For Tom, in memoriam

Holy Days of Obligation

Remember for Me

~

When my father died it was spring, lilacs the strongest smell, and enough sun to begin to grow real tomatoes to replace the pale, woody ones we'd eaten all winter. "Bring me a tomato sandwich," my father ordered from his hospital bed, his face grey, two flushed spots on his cheeks. "I want it toasted! And make the toast dark," he told us as we left to make the sandwich in the patients' kitchen. "Lots of butter. Dripping. And lots of mayonnaise and pepper. Don't let your mother salt it; she uses too much."

He managed to eat a bite or two, Catherine holding it up to his mouth, before he offered it to us. We said no. Even though we knew we couldn't catch cancer, this was the sandwich of a dying man.

"Will you roll at my funeral, too?" he asked.

We'd rolled down the hill at the cemetery when our brother, Robert, was buried. The ground was cold, covered with pathetic wisps of November-browned grass. No one answered when my father asked because my mother began to cry, but it was understood, just by his asking, that we would.

~

I thought I'd be relieved when my father died. He would stop suffering and I could stop watching him suffer. I also thought I'd be rid of his silences, and his orders, advice and guilt. No such luck. While he was alive I ignored him, or argued. After he died it wasn't that easy. For weeks he moved inside my head like a re-run on television.

He would have liked that about TV. Not a day went by that my father didn't watch the North American minimum, probably the average. And on weekends he worked his damnedest to help get that average raised. When he was older TV was like a sedative. Turn it on and he turned off, head tilted sideways and not quite resting on his shoulder. We never woke him.

But when he was younger he watched with enthusiasm and passion, talking to the set, moving his arms, shaking his head, cigarette smoke snorting out of his nostrils when he laughed.

I said to him, "It's second-hand living, Dad. Why don't you *go* to the game or go to *see* the show? Why don't you *do* something?" My father would say, "Look at that. Will you just take one look at that, Bertha." He'd be watching a show on dolphins—Jacques Cousteau probably—or about Africa. Or news specials. He especially liked those.

When the news broadcasts showed the first lunar landing, my father was there, home early from work, beer opened, a fresh pack of cigarettes waiting to be christened. He was *with* Armstrong, Aldrin and Collins when Neil Armstrong's ghostly figure descended from the Eagle onto the moon. "That's one small step for man, one giant leap for mankind,"Armstrong said to my father.

"Who'd have thought," my father said to Armstrong on the flickering screen, "that I'd be alive to see a man on the moon!"

When John Kennedy was killed, my father cried with Walter Cronkite because Kennedy was Irish Catholic and from a large family and so were we, though only part Irish on his mother's side. That was where the resemblance ended. The Kennedys were wealthy, lived in mansions and compounds, had boats and big cars. We were eleven people living in a three-bedroom bungalow in a suburb in a Southern Ontario industrial town. I pointed this out to him.

"Television has no borders," he said, "and it's equal. Everyone gets the same shows, rich or poor." He turned away from the screen to look at me. "Grief is equal too," he added.

Cronkite wasn't there when my father died; nor was my father's oldest son, Robert. Robert had committed suicide. Besides me—Bertha to my father, Bertie to everyone else—there were Catherine, Margaret, David, Veronica, Michael, Sandra and Simon, in that order, Robert coming between Margaret and David when he lived. And our mother, Elizabeth. And our husbands, wives, lovers and kids, of course. The hospital corridors were full and noisy, the smell of cigarette smoke strong on those who'd gone down to the lounge where we were surprised to find smoking was still permitted.

My father didn't have a quiet death; he had company until the moment he died. If he got tired of us he'd glare around the room and say, "This is something a man must do alone. None of *you* will be coming with me." And he'd turn on his side and pretend to sleep. But if we left him alone too long, one of us would arrive to find his food tray sitting untouched and cold, or his bedclothes soaked with urine, and my father's eyes filled with reproach.

We'd wash him and change the bed, lean his frail body against our hips, strip sheets from one side, then the other. "Remember for me about fishing?" he'd ask when we were done.

~

They need worms for fishing, and Bertha's father, Frank, always knows where to find them. Now Bertha, his oldest daughter, knows too. This is what she's learned: look in shady places where the leaves from last year have collected and are rotting; look in the corners of the fence and along its bottom rail; also under rocks in the rock garden, or over beside the green metal shed where the leaky bags of garbage have been stored until garbage day for years.

The smell of the earth that holds worms is rich and tinny, the smell of dampness after a summer rain. Bertha calls it "the smell of worms." "It smells like worms out here," she calls to her brothers and sisters as they run across the lawn in their bare feet leaving flattened green trails on the silver-drenched grass.

Leftover worms have another smell. "High," Frank calls them as he holds the container, an old blue Player's tobacco tin with holes punched into the lid, straight out and away from his nose. "Just plain laziness," he mutters. Then louder, "Who didn't put these back in the garden?"

Of course Bertha isn't going to admit that it's her fault. Never anyone's really, but she has a feeling, from the way he says it—thin-lipped, grim and slow—that each yard has a quota of worms that will certainly run out if she doesn't put the ones they haven't used back into the garden.

Frank is right. Sometimes Bertha can't find any worms no matter where she looks. Then she goes to their neighbour, her father's friend, Vern Snyder. He loves to fish, but only with men. He tells her where to find worms in his yard and she never takes more than she needs.

And Bertha always returns leftover worms to Mr. Snyder's garden. She knocks at his door, tells him what she is doing, holds the container up so he can see. He asks her what they caught and she tells him sunfish, maybe a half-dozen little trout, sometimes a bass or two. She tells him in detail because he likes to know; he listens and he asks the right questions: who caught what; were they using kids' poles or Frank's new rod; were they using lures, or a sinker and bobber; were the bugs bad, and most important of all, had they caught any fish with the worms from his garden?

Mr. Snyder is broad-chested, tall. He combs his hair, which shines with oil, straight up at the sides and into a high rounded curlicue in the front. He rocks back and forth when he talks. After a while Bertha feels as though she is swaying to his rhythm. Back and forth. His words seem to reach her from close up, far away, close up again. Back and forth as though his voice is being carried on an imperceptible breeze.

He likes to know that Bertha'd caught some of the fish with his worms. He winks and tells her maybe he should get half of the catch. His share. She tells him that means he gets only one fish because the others were small and her father made her throw them back in, except the one Simon got hold of and squished and pulled until all of the fish's slime came off. Bertha knows that a trout can't live without its slime. Her father had shown her a sick fish that wasn't able to swim properly because it had been caught, over-handled, then thrown back into the water to die a cruel and needless death, he said.

She learned that if she damages a fish it is better to give it a tap on the head with the handle of the fish knife, or a rock, and later bury it in the garden to make fertilizer and more worms. She tries to remember where she plants those dead fish so she can dig the worms that are supposed to grow from them. She never seems to be able to find the fish graves and the new worms that should be spawning.

Her mother, Elizabeth, says it is all foolishness anyway, planting fish. Some old cat will come along and dig up her marigolds and portulaca trying to find the rotten things. It will spray its foul scent everywhere along with its poop, which Simon, the baby, will probably dig up and eat. "Then we'll have worms," she says, "more worms than we ever wanted, that's for sure." That is her opinion on worms and dead fish, for all it seems to matter. For all anyone listens.

"Or cares," she adds after a pause.

Bertha giggles when her mother says "poop" and looks over at her father who shakes his head until her mother is finished what she is saying. Then he sends Bertha to get the shovel and find a good place to bury the fish.

~

Once the old tobacco tin of worms is packed with the right amount of rotted leaves and placed in the cooler, they're off. Frank's favourite fishing hole is out past Rosedale. This is the route as Bertha remembers it: drive through Kitchener to Bridgeport past The Casino, the dance hall that Bertha thinks must be both elegant and risqué. She has never been there. It is on the hill to her right. To her left is Gingrich's Dairy, which everyone calls Glupse's for no reason anyone ever knows. They just always have, her mother tells her. They'll return there for homemade ice-cream in crispy cones on their way home.

At the bottom of the hill is the corner where the old bachelor called "The General" directs traffic, wearing his winter clothing no matter what season it is. If Bertha's grandmother is with them they will joke about her marrying "The General" now that she is a widow. This makes her laugh. "The General" holds a handmade STOP sign. The family becomes quiet as they pass, as though "The General" has the power to hear them through the metal of the car. Bertha turns to watch him as her father turns right. When "The General" is out of sight she speculates on how he lives, how he must smell, how she would be his friend if she lived in Bridgeport.

Within seconds they are in the country and the fields and elm trees with tall broad crowns whiz by. The car windows are rolled down and the smells are of dust, cow manure, and the sweetness of cut hay. At Rosedale Corner Frank turns right again, drives past the house Bertha's mother grew up in—smaller now, it seems, or so her mother says—and down an old concrete road beside the new bridge.

The road comes to an abrupt end. The cliff falls straight down to the water, which is low. Old pylons stand at intervals across the river. Frank finds the path and walks the older children to the deeper fishing holes while Elizabeth sets out blankets and play things for the younger ones. As the oldest, Bertha is allowed to wade over to the pylons. The sun brings out the smell of old, wet cement.

Bertha goes to the shady side of the pylon where she looks deep into the water. A fish emerges from the shadows; sun lights the rainbow on its side. It moves as slowly as time when it is forgotten. The sounds of the water...the picnic...the traffic...recede. Bertha concentrates on the spot where the fish sways in the current. She breathes the cement and water smells which are so strong they are not like air at all, but something dense and almost solid. Warmth makes her feel weak, and her breathing is matched to the rhythm of the fish's gills. Breathe in. And out. In. Out. The water is still, and contained. In. Out. Then the fish darts away so quickly she gasps. She doubts her eyes. She searches the water for the fish but can't find it again.

Noises return; the water appears to move; Bertha notices a breeze. The thick damp mustiness changes to the yeasty smell of beer or bread. When Bertha reaches the blanket where her mother sits with the napping baby, her mother says they'll eat in fifteen minutes. She always says that, as though fifteen minutes is exactly the right amount of time to wait for anything: a conversation to end, a chore to be done, a baby to finish sleeping. The right amount of time before something new can begin, something not yet defined by action, not too urgent but necessary just the same.

Bertha fishes while she waits to eat. She wears old sneakers so the stones won't hurt her feet. The sharp coldness of the water penetrates the canvas and rushes into the holes at the sides and toes of the shoes. A fine brown silt catches on the hairs on her legs, minnows nibble at her shoes.

Someone gets sunburned and the smell of Noxzema mixes with those of the picnic: sandwiches (egg salad and peanut butter and jam on soft white bread), beer and lemonade, cookies (two kinds) and sticky squares, coffee, a Thermos full of warm milk for the baby, raw vegetables floating in ice water, a bag of ripe black cherries. And someone, David probably, drops part of his sandwich into the water and begins to cry. Elizabeth says it doesn't matter (they all feel the specialness of the reprieve), that she has made more sandwiches than they need. There is only exactly the right amount in the end, though.

Bertha throws her crusts to the fish, watches as they rise to the surface to feed, then disappear in darts and dashes of whirling reflected light and tiny eddies. After the picnic, bloated bits of crust lodge in the pebbles and rocks along the edge of the water, bob until the current catches them and draws them into the river's flow.

At this point, Frank picks up his rod and leaves to fish in the deepest water. The pool he chooses appears slow moving, benign, and is dark and glossy. Bertha watches him. She can't see his line but sees the slow movement of his arm as it reaches back the exact right distance then comes forward in a clean fast snap which sets his lure spinning in the sunshine. It falls in what Bertha thinks must be the best place for a line to fall—the place she'd want her line to fall if she were fishing with him. He reels the line in slowly, and casts over and over again as though he is practising for perfection or thinks he will actually catch a fish. By the time he returns the car is packed and they are ready to go home.

SUNBURN

Cliff Gibson pulls his car into the driveway that separates his lawn from Frank's. Frank is in the back seat with Vern Snyder. Vern's brother Gus is in the front seat with Cliff. Gus needed to be in the front because he was feeling fragile, having drunk too much rye over the weekend. There is a line of dried vomit that starts at Gus' window, runs across Frank's and straight down to the back of the car; Gus stuck his head out to get sick as they drove along the highway. Frank is a bit embarrassed about this, hates the smell too, but doesn't let on. His feet hurt enough to distract him from the smell and the mess.

The motor coughs twice, then stops. As he opens his door, Frank winces. He turns, lifts both feet over the edge of the door frame and gingerly places them, side by side, flat down onto the asphalt. He can feel the heat from the pavement right through his shoes. He leans forward at the waist, grabs onto the frame and hoists himself up. Frank never swears, rarely blasphemes, but he is close to it today.

Already the children are around him and he hopes they will not accidentally trample his feet. Not even bump them gently.

"How many fish did you catch? Are there any big ones? Daddy, did you catch any? What's that smell?"

The sound of their voices mingles with the thud of the car doors as they are closed, Gus' groan as he settles into a lawn chair on Cliff's front porch, the tick of the car's cooling engine, the whine and slap of screen doors as the women come out of the houses and gather around the edges of the crowd. Frank looks down, concentrates so hard on his sore feet, that he hears these sounds distinctly as though they are happening inside his head instead of outside it. He looks up and sees Elizabeth, his wife, standing beside Cliff's wife, Helen. Veronica, Frank's youngest child, is wedged on Elizabeth's hip. Elizabeth smiles at him, concern showing in the lift of an eyebrow.

"I sunburned my feet."

He says this above the noise of the children. He says this to Elizabeth only. He moves to step toward her and winces again. She winces too, looks down at his feet, looks up and mouths, "How?" But there is the hint of a smile at the edges of her lips. She shakes her head and looks down again. Frank knows she is laughing.

Elizabeth's smile disappears. Frank sees her look around, spin her body in an agitated sweep, Veronica almost tipping out of her arms. She is looking at all of the children gathered around the car.

"Frank, do you see David? David! DAVID! Kids, help me find David."

Frank groans as he watches the children begin the search in a delighted, chaotic way.

David is their three-year-old hellion. He learned to walk early, climbed everything, including the doorways, which he scaled by placing a foot on each side of the frame and inching one foot then the other upwards. David dropped Plasticine down the heating vents and tried to stick bobby pins into the electrical sockets. He broke his leg when he was one—fell out of the high chair. Slipped out of the harness, slouched downward then slid onto the floor, his arms pointed up in the air. He screamed when he landed. He didn't stop screaming until they'd put him out at the hospital to set his leg. Not one of the other first four kids, nor the one after, had got out of that harness!

Even the cast didn't slow David down. He loved to make noise, so he crawled as fast as he could, skirting carpets and sticking to the bare hardwood floors. A bump was followed by a loud thump. Bump-THUMP, bump-THUMP, bump-THUMP. He'd stop, sit on his bum, look around at his audience. The other children adored David, and when he laughed and clapped his hands at his own performance, they laughed and clapped too.

"I bet there're still dents in my hardwood floors from that cast."

"What's that, Frank?"

Vern has a handful of fishing poles. He extracts Frank's and hands it to him. Frank reaches out, takes it in his hand. The handle swings over and hits his foot. His lips pull into a firm thin line.

"It's David. Elizabeth can't find him. Guess I'd better give her a hand. I'll get my stuff in a few minutes, Vern."

"I'll help look, too."

Vern—the whole neighbourhood, for that matter—knows about David. Vern takes Frank's pole and leans it with the rest against the car.

"Cliff, come help Frank find David. He got away from Elizabeth again."

Elizabeth sticks her head out of the doorway.

"Frank, get in here. David's locked himself in the bathroom. I can't get him to open the door."

Elizabeth disappears. Vern and Cliff cut straight over the lawn and into Frank's house. The screen door slaps wildly behind them. WHAP-WHAP-WHAP! Frank's lips get thinner.

"I'll have to fix that," he says out loud to no one.

Frank hobbles as quickly as he can on his swollen feet. He stops, sits on the grass and very slowly takes off a running shoe. He can't stand the way it rubs the blisters on his skin.

"Feels like sandpaper," he mutters.

Even the long blades of grass that brush the sides of his now bare foot feel like razors slicing at the too tender skin.

"Fishing. Fishing. Think about the fishing, Frank." He says this to himself, under his breath.

Frank struggles with a knot in the lace of the other shoe and remembers how clear the weather was on Saturday morning. Clear *and* warm. A steady light breeze kept the worst of the bugs away without disturbing the fish or making the casting difficult. They had breakfast at the camp, plus a splash of rye in their coffee. No reason not to. Just to get them going. Vern splashed rye onto his hands, too, then onto his face like aftershave.

"It'll either kill the damn bugs or they'll go away happy," he said.

Gus must have had a few extra shots at breakfast that Frank didn't notice, because he was asleep under a tree fifteen minutes after his first cast hit the water. In fact Gus stayed hammered or sleeping it off for the whole trip, then vomited all the way home in the car. Frank didn't have a whole lot of sympathy for him, that's for sure.

Cliff and Vern crossed the river and walked a half-mile up to the old willow pool. Frank decided to fish along the shore. With Gus asleep, the only sounds came from the water as it ran over the rocks, the breeze as it whispered through the eel grass, and the whirl and plonk of his line as he cast it into the deeper pools. Every once in a while Frank heard the men shout:

"Slow! Bring it in slow. No, no, let some line go. Shit. Where's that net? Oh, it's a beaut, it's a real beaut."

Always pretty much the same. Always everything said twice like a demented echo. Gus lifted his head, grunted, "Atta boy, atta boy," when he heard the shouts, then fell asleep again.

Frank fished in a pair of old holey canvas running shoes. His waders leaked and had got too brittle to patch anymore. Couldn't afford new ones, with all the kids, fixing up the basement as the girls' bedroom and, maybe, trying to do a holiday at a cottage this summer, too. Bertha, his oldest, was thirteen and had never had a family vacation away from home. He'd make a go of it if Elizabeth was game. Borrow some money from the Credit Union. Kids and debts, he had plenty of both.

Frank looked over at Gus, whose legs were stretched out like shiny, smooth frogs' legs, spread wide at the crotch, bent at the knee, dappled as the sun shone on them through the leaves of a tree. Gus could've lent Frank his waders. But Gus didn't offer. And Frank never asked. Never would.

Heat built around Frank's head and shoulders. It mixed with the tinny smell of earthworms and water, and the sweetness of bruised grasses at the river side. He let his line fly, listened to the whir and zip as it moved through the air.

Frank took a break to have a smoke and dry out a bit. He imagined that his feet must be like albino prunes. He lit a cigarette and blew the smoke at the blackflies that began to bother him. He held the cigarette in the side of his mouth, squinting through the smoke. He undid his laces, pulled a wet shoe off with a popping whoosh as he broke the suction of water holding the shoe to his bare foot. He tossed the shoe aside and looked at his foot and a wave of faintness passed through him. He took his cigarette, drew on it hard, blew the smoke at his toes. He leaned forward and placed the hot tip onto the leech that lay long, flat and black across the indentations of four of his toes. It sizzled and pulled into itself, lifted off his skin. Frank flicked the leech into the grass. He took another hard drag from the cigarette and touched the second leech that curled over the toenail of his big toe. It too sizzled. He pulled phlegm and bile from his throat into his mouth and spat it in the direction he had flicked the leeches.

Frank's toenail was softened and fleshy where the leech had started to dissolve it, sucking for blood. He rubbed it to remove the slime. He finished his cigarette and decided to fish in bare feet, standing in the sandy shallows. He could see what was going on with his feet then.

That's how he got the sunburn. He fished the rest of the day barefoot at the edge of the river, his tender white feet exposed to the sun. At five he knew they were burned; by suppertime he couldn't even taste the feed of rainbow trout that Vern fried up in butter. He was too distracted by the cooking of his skin as it swelled and began to blister. When he crawled into his sleeping bag, dizzy from too much rye, the pain remained. In the middle of the night he unzipped his bag, stuck his feet outside because the brush of the soft flannel lining was too much. When it touched the hairs on his toes, his feet twitched with a prickling pain.

~

Frank tosses his shoes onto his porch and pulls the screen door handle. The hardwood floor in the hallway feels cool. Everyone in the neighbourhood will know the sunburn part of his story soon enough, but the leeches part he'll save for Elizabeth. He'd purposely not told Vern and Cliff about those leeches, and he'd never have told Gus. He'll tell her tonight. In bed. He can hear her groan, then begin to laugh at what happened. She'll help him figure out how he is going to get his feet into work boots tomorrow morning. But right now he has to find his screwdriver to unbolt the lock on the bathroom door. It isn't the first time one of the kids has locked themselves in, but with David you never know, you just never know what will happen next.

Frank hears Elizabeth and Vern trying to talk David into unlocking the door. David is crying. Screaming actually. Over this he can hear the sound of water running.

"Turn the water off, David. Listen, sweetheart, do as Mommy says. It's OK. Just turn the water off and open the door."

"How long has the water been running, Elizabeth?"

Elizabeth does not turn to look at Frank but continues to talk to the door handle.

"I don't know. Daddy's here now, David. He'll help you open the door."

Frank bends over and loosens the screws at the sides of the lock. Water is seeping under the door, but not too much. It is cold, and after the first shock is almost pleasant.

"This water is freezing. Are you sure you don't know how long it's been running?"

No one answers. Elizabeth, Vern and Cliff stand back from the door as Frank loosens the last screw. Frank kneels, reaches to grab the door handle as it comes away from the wood and falls into his hands. He sets it on the floor. David is quiet; the water noise is loud. He pulls the door wide and runs straight into his father. He takes one step back, says, "Daddy?" His eyes are dark and look over Frank's shoulder at Elizabeth. He begins screaming again. Frank lifts him straight up holding him at the shoulders. He turns, hands him to Elizabeth.

"Put him in his room. Make him shut up."

Frank sees that David has put the plug in the sink, then turned the water on. Frank pulls the plug and turns the faucet off. Soaking wet towels and the bath mat are wedged along the bottom of the door, which explains why so little water came out that way. Most of the water has run straight down along the bottom edges of the toilet and the bathtub. Frank realizes that it must be gathering in the basement below.

"My room." Frank whispers this.

"My room! The girls' bedroom!" He begins to shout. "Elizabeth, the water. It's going into my brand new room!"

Frank looks at Vern, then Cliff. Elizabeth runs to the bathroom. The three men push past her and run toward the basement.

Vern turns and bumps into Elizabeth who has started to follow.

"I'll get our mop. Cliff, go get yours," Elizabeth says.

They leave. The screen door whaps behind them. Frank limps as fast as he can down the stairs, slams his foot into some pop bottles left on the landing and howls.

"E-LIZ-A-BETH!"

The door to the girls' new bedroom is closed. Two inches of water cover the cement in the rest of the basement. Frank opens the door and a rush of water pours out. By the time it levels there is a three-inch covering of water everywhere. The worst of the flow is coming from the ceiling tiles directly under the bathroom, right over Bertha's bed. Frank pushes the bed out of the way. It is heavy and the bedding is dark and soggy.

Vern and Cliff arrive, wearing their hip waders, carrying scrub mops and pails. Elizabeth, who has been standing at the door, walks into the room in her leather shoes, which spurt a funnel of water up from the instep every time she sets her foot down. She looks around the room, starts to back out, her hands pushed deep into the pockets of her apron.

"Oh, Frank," she says. "Oh poor, poor Frank. Your room."

Frank watches her until she is gone. He doesn't say another word. Not one. Cliff and Vern begin to mop up, trying to push water out the door toward the drain in the laundry room. Cliff slushes his way out, following the path the water should be taking but isn't.

"It's capped, Frank."

Cliff returns to the bedroom holding the brand new twist-on cap Frank had installed on the drain to stop the kids from sticking Tinkertoys through the holes of the old one, yet allow Elizabeth to open the drain when she needed to do the laundry. Frank only grunts. The water level begins to go down.

Frank presses on one of the soggy white ceiling tiles that he had just finished installing the week before. A perfect white tile, twelve inches square, fitting neatly into the tiles that surround it. He pushes until the tile cracks away from its staples. A torrent of water runs down, soaking him. Cliff begins to laugh, but stops abruptly. Frank is not smiling. With the cold water flowing away, Frank's sore bare feet begin to hurt again.

The three men work until most of the water is gone. Damp spots show everywhere. They haul the mattress outside to dry, and Elizabeth hangs the bedding on the line. An audience of children has gathered along the edges of the window well to watch the basement clean-up. They are silent as they watch, run away to giggle in the corner of the yard, and return subdued and grim-faced, just like Frank. David has fallen asleep on his bed, Elizabeth reports, when she brings the men some beer to try to lighten things up.

Frank kneels to wipe up one last pool of water. He almost caresses the floor tiles he still hasn't paid for. When the bill is paid, Elizabeth will file it in the ledger in the top drawer of their dresser. Right now the bill is sitting on the kitchen counter waiting for a loan instalment to come through.

Soft lines like sadness appear around Frank's mouth. He remembers coming down to finish wiring the sockets and screw the plates into place. The girls—Bertha, Catherine and Margaret—had been sprawled out on their stomachs, passing a magnifying glass from one to the other.

"What are you doing?"

"We're seeing if this here's real gold, Daddy. If it is, we're rich, aren't we?"

He'd laughed and laughed. "Oh, I wish, girls, I just wish."

The floor tiles are white with clear acrylic pools of floating gold glitter embedded in them. He liked them from the moment he saw them in the building supply store, and so did Elizabeth. The water won't damage them, but all the new wood underneath will take days to dry, maybe weeks.

Frank looks up. Elizabeth is watching from the doorway; Veronica is back on her hip.

"Hope the weather holds."

"Frank?"

"Said, hope the weather holds 'til this is all dried out. Where are the kids?"

"Helen's feeding them hot dogs from the barbecue. She's saving some for you fellows too. Why don't you go now while they're still warm? I'll help out here."

Elizabeth holds Veronica with one arm and reaches with the other to touch Frank's hand, then lifts it to say good-bye to Cliff and Vern.

"Helen's going to keep the girls tonight, until we get things dried up some. It'll be okay."

"I know. It's just that I only finished Thursday and this is Sunday. It's not even *paid* for, Elizabeth, and it's wrecked. And look at these feet. How am I supposed to get my boots on and go in to work tomorrow?"

Frank stands looking down at his feet, which are wrinkled along the sides and bright red with blisters that are grossly swollen across the top. Elizabeth looks down at them too. She just shakes her head.

~

Frank and Elizabeth go to bed after midnight. David wouldn't settle down after sleeping in the afternoon. Frank talked to him, told him everything was okay, but never, *ever,* do that again. David started whimpering. Then he wanted to play. Frank was willing. He had a special feeling for David, a combination of aggravation and admiration.

Frank leans over onto his elbow and turns to face Elizabeth. Elizabeth is lying on her back under the sheet. Frank can tell that she's awake. He starts to tell her about the leeches and the sunburn.

"Eliz..."

"Frank, I'm going to see Dr. Ritchie tomorrow. I wanted to wait until after the fishing trip, after the girls' room was finished, to tell you."

She turns on her side and faces Frank.

"Are you sure? I thought you had a period last month."

"No. That was just some spotting. Nothing came of it. I'm pretty sure, Frank. In fact, I'm positive."

They lie together facing each other. Their bodies do not touch. Frank sits up and yanks the sheet out from the end of the bed, tucks it around his legs and leaves his feet out. He lies back with a thump. Some of the blisters on his feet have broken. Clear fluid oozes out and dries in patches and crusty dribbles on his skin.

"Good night, Frank."

In all their married life Frank has always kissed Elizabeth good night. Except, that is, when she's in hospital having babies or he is away fishing. Tonight he's not going to do it. He won't make a habit of *not* kissing her, he knows this already, but just this once he is not going to kiss Elizabeth good night.

He thinks of her nipples, knows their look during pregnancy—large and dark, almost bluish-black. He begins to reach for her. His feet bump together. The pain makes him suck in his breath. Not tonight. Damn it to hell, not tonight. And he won't tell her about the leeches either, maybe not ever, but definitely not now.

WATCH

I sometimes wonder how my father sees me. I have to squint to see myself. Maybe because I am so skinny. Tall—5'10" at seventeen—and fair too. I feel as if I'm more eyes and ears than anything else. Some days I look in the mirror to try to connect the pieces of my face to one another, but what I see are eyes looking at eyes looking at eyes. Or I see what I am that's like him, and think: these brown eyes are fine, his are smoky blue, but I'd like to have a more definite chin line. (Here I lift my chin far up on my neck and press the skin under my jaw tight into my throat. I hold it until I think I'll choke, then let go.) And a longer neck, a less sharp nose than mine and his.

What else I have from him is my name, Bertha. It's really from an aunt he loved, he says, who gave him hard maple candy whenever he visited her. She was short and dark. I hate maple candy. The name also came from a saint who'd been rich, had only one child and gave away all of her money to the poor. "For God's sake," I like to say to him when he shows me this story in the book of saints. My father hates blaspheming. I call myself Bertie. My father doesn't.

What I do have that's mine is this: a full-time summer job at Vogel's store (part-time during school) that pays enough to indulge my passion for buying shoes and presents, like the toaster oven I got my mother for her birthday, with some left over for my savings account marked "Nurse's Training Savings." Blonde hair that feels good, shines in the sun, and is long enough to flick over my shoulder. It even stays there.

A best friend named Karen whom I should be planning to go roller skating with at the Glenbriar right now. She has 38B breasts with smooth, dark brown nipples, a flat stomach, hips like a boy's. She has more boyfriends than she wants, she says, and wears false eyelashes to roller skating just for fun. She even has a pair made from mink fur that are self-adhesive and so thick they don't need mascara. Her eyes are small and fur lashes make them look frightened and tired. I've never told her this.

I also have a driver's licence, and a brand new pair of white cotton duck Bermuda shorts. I bought them from Sommer's Ladies' Wear for this very holiday that we are on. They were full price, but the saleswoman, Rita, gave them to me at 25% off because I was leaving town for nurse's training.

Rita has dyed red hair teased up at least three inches on the top. It's so stiff with hairspray it shifts as a whole if it moves at all. Sommer's sells traditional women's clothes on the main floor and up-to-date juniors' in the basement down a narrow set of wooden stairs that smell like lemon oil and ironing. Rita works in the basement, but always wears upstairs clothes—a straight skirt with a slit up the back, a kitten sweater set with a sweater clip and red lipstick that leaves traces on her teeth. When she sold me the shorts she said, "Nurse's training. Why don't you go to university? Don't go away to learn how to clean up messes after sick people. Be something! Your poor mother's going to miss you."

~

I'm wearing the shorts now on this hottest day of the year. They're probably wrinkled because my legs are stuck to the hot vinyl seat covering and because my brother, Robert, has been sitting on my lap for the last twenty minutes. His sweaty, fat legs push the material into bunches and their sticky dampness practically strips the skin off my thighs every time he shifts to look out window. There are twelve people in the car—my parents, myself, four sisters and four brothers all younger than I, and my maternal grandmother whom I adore. I begged off work to go on this, my last family holiday to a cottage called "Happy Ours" at Sauble Beach.

We have a full-sized, three-seat station wagon. Even when completely loaded with all our gear and the roof rack full, it rides up high on the suspension. The car was driving just fine, but now begins to lose power. My father, who talks to me about cars because I'm the only one in my family who drives or is even remotely interested, looks for my eyes in the rearview mirror.

"I think it's the gas pump or something in the gas line, Bertha. It gets these surges then slows down. I give it all the gas I can, then my foot's on the floor again and nothing happens. We had that trouble one other time, remember?"

I do, but it isn't really a question. My father just needs to say something because he's not the swearing type. I know, if the trouble gets worse, he'll become silent. His mouth will set in a firm line pulling all his anger into tiny wrinkles that appear sewn into his lips like darts into a dress. As I grow older I find myself angry in silence too. I feel, in my skin, that my father's face becomes impressed on my own. I have to open my mouth, say some words to ease the lines so that my face no longer feels the way my father's looks.

My father doesn't say another word about the car.

I turn my eyes away from the mirror, where I can still see his face, to look at my mother who sits in the front seat, the baby on her lap and my sister between them and my father. My mother, too, remains silent on the subject of the car, putting all of her energy into keeping the children quiet and seated. The car moves in a roller coaster motion, first speeding along, then almost slowing to a stop before it surges violently forward again.

"What's that, Mommy? Why's the car doing that? I'm thirsty. Daddy, when do we get to the cottage?"

"Sh," my mother says. "Bertie, would you get your brother's arm in from out of the window?"

My mother's tone is gentle. Tired. As always asking something that she seems to think is impossible.

My grandmother remains quiet, too, having learned to let my mother handle these situations in her own way. My grandmother is proud of the fact that she's come to look after us children every time my mother has gone to the hospital to have a baby. She'd start out doing everything—baking, mending, even ironing the underwear. By the end of the week she'd be exhausted and short-tempered.

Once she said to me, "I hope your father has the sense to stay away from her for awhile. This is too much work for any human being."

I remember every word. I hear it in my head. After each baby is born I understand more.

When my grandmother repeated this sentiment to my mother, after she had come home from the hospital, my mother asked her, "Which of these children would you have me get rid of? Which one should I not have had?"

My grandmother took this newest baby in her arms while my mother hung up her coat and talked to each now older child. We all went into my parents' bedroom where my grandmother placed the baby on the chenille bedspread. My mother sat on the edge of the bed and showed the baby: hair like one of us, fingers long like another's, this the cord where the baby got his food. It would fall off in a week or so. We laughed and said yes, yes. My grandmother's voice was the loudest and happiest, this being the longest, fattest, prettiest one so far. But when she said these things, when I saw her eyes look at my father, they looked dark and hard. Just like they do now, every time the car slows.

"We passed a garage a ways back, Daddy. Maybe we should turn around."

I try not to sound whiny in case it makes my father more determined to go on. There's no need. The car motor comes to a complete stop. The wind from the open windows diminishes and heats up. All of the children hush at once. As we roll along all we hear is the crunch of each and every piece of gravel the tires touch as my father manoeuvers the car to the side of the road.

~

My father remains in his seat. Both of his hands are on the steering wheel, one at ten o'clock and one at two, just as he had showed me when he taught me how to drive. I notice his neck is sunburned. Some of the pores on it are enlarged; one has a deep core of black that is raised slightly above the skin level with a distinct, whitened ridge around it. I want to lean forward and squeeze it out, but instead, jiggle my brother's legs up and down to try to cool off our thighs. I can't take my eyes off my father's neck though. There are also two lines of curly auburn hair growing down both sides of his neck that disappear into the collar of his clean white T-shirt. Without moving his head, only his shoulders, he reaches down and pulls the hood-release knob. The hood thumps open and in one motion he opens his door, is out and walking around to the front of the car.

Inside the car, heat and noise explode. I get out to see what my father will do. I stand as close to him as I can because he seems not to notice that I'm here. He touches the hoses, the gas line, hits a hot spot and sucks in his breath, pulls his hand away, shakes it, touches it to his lips. He checks the battery connections. I look at his mouth, watch it tighten. Much as I wish he would say something, I know he won't.

"May as well get out and take the kids over there into the shade, Mom."

I lean my head into my mother's window as I talk to her. I can smell the sour cheesy white spot on the shoulder of her blouse where the baby has spit up. My mother has smelled this way for as long as I have known her.

"He's pretty quiet. I don't think he's got this one figured out and he's sure not looking for help."

I jerk my head in the direction of my father, almost wishing that he'd overhear. I'm about to stand up when the baby grabs my hair in his relentless, non-release grip. I start to frown but give him my biggest smile instead. He responds as he always does: an open-mouthed, toothless grin full of drool and laughter. I can't imagine my father ever being a baby but the thought makes me laugh. What I do imagine is his face, as it is now, on a baby's body. The baby laughs even louder as though he knows what I'm thinking and is having the same thought. That's the way it is with this baby.

~

I love this baby differently than I love my other brothers and sisters. I can't resist touching him whenever I'm near him; his skin is tight and smooth as an apple. But warm. I like his milky breath and the way his fingernails and his hair grow. And how he'll fall asleep in my arms with his mouth open, head leaning back, after I feed him his bottle. I sometimes think he is mine. That I made him. And that's the crunch. I could have made him.

Before, when my mother got pregnant, she just did and was. At some point we'd notice, place our hands on the stretched elastic over her belly and feel it move. She'd go away for a week and come home with a baby. There was no surprise, except for the time her waters broke when she was taking a roast out of the oven. We all laughed because our mother had had an accident on the kitchen floor. This is what I remember: she went to the bathroom, got a towel and put it over the wet spot. She served us supper, sometimes stopping to hold onto the edge of the stove or the table. While we ate, she cleaned up the mess on the floor, then went to lie down in the bedroom. After my father finished eating, he called my grandmother to come in a taxi, told me to clean up the supper dishes, which I resented, and took my mother to the hospital. She came home a week later with my sister Veronica.

The difference with the last baby was that I knew, from the beginning, how the baby was conceived. And my mother knew I knew. She took me aside before she was even showing and told me, "I'm pregnant. The baby will be born in February, probably the second week. I wanted you to be the first to know. I'll need your help, Bertie." At first I just said sure, and was she going to tell the other kids. She said no, she was going to wait awhile. As I digested the news I began to understand. My parents went all the way. Had been for years, in the bedroom across the hall from mine and my sisters'.

I knew what it was like, almost. I had made out before, kissed until my panties were wet and sticky. I had felt a hard penis rub on my leg, up and down, over and over again, pressing and pressing. My breasts had been touched and the sensations had connected with my groin, making it tight and aching, throbbing with too much blood. I had never gone all the way, but my parents had. Watching my mother's breasts grow heavy and her stomach swell was enough to slow me down. This was not going to happen to me for a long, long time.

When my mother began to go into labour she told me what was happening. I could see her huge belly tighten and seem to get longer and thinner, but that could have been in my mind. She lifted her top and said, "Touch it. Go ahead, now, while it's contracting." I did. It was harder than any skin I'd ever felt, even harder than the muscle in my father's arm when he flexed it. Harder by far than the boy's penis that I had felt on my leg, that I'd reached down to touch once or twice.

And when my mother brought this baby home, I felt I knew him better than the rest. When my grandmother said this was the best baby yet, I was inclined to agree. I watched closely. I loved him and saw him take as much as my mother and everyone else had to give. Babies are like that.

Several weeks before this holiday that we are supposed to be on, I also watched and helped my mother nurse herself and the rest of us through a bout of stomach flu. I noticed darkness around my mother's eyes and a lined heaviness at the edges of her mouth. We were doing the dishes—my mother, myself, and my sisters. I rubbed the dish towel round and round a plate with a faded rose pattern. I felt each bubble along the edge, let my fingernails pop over each one, making a noise like a dripping faucet.

"I'm never going to have children."

"Oh, Bertie." Her voice was thick and low. She didn't look at me. "Why?"

I stood still. I tried to think why. I knew I had to answer and more than that I wanted to. I wanted her to know I saw everything.

"I never want to be like you."

I was looking straight ahead. Even so, in the distance that separated us at the sink, I felt her body pull away from mine.

"You might change your mind someday."

I didn't answer.

~

Now I want to protect my mother.

"I'll get the blankets out of the back of the car. You and Grandma can go to that patch of grass. I'll be over in a minute."

My father is standing by the side of the car. He is not moving, though his image wavers in the heat shimmering up in waves from the car engine in front of him and the pavement behind. I help the children to the grassy places, carry one, take another by the hand, and tell them where they can play and where they can't.

"See that line over there where the grass starts to get stony? Don't go past that line."

I spread the old plaid car blanket over the tall grass. A smell like oil and stale bread rises with it and seems not to settle even when the blanket does. The heat has caught and held it like an invisible cloud above the surface of the cloth. My grandmother and mother sit down on it and the smell of bruised grasses sweetens the air around them. I walk back to the car, each step in the heat like trying to shift a weight with my legs.

"What are you going to do?"

As I ask this, I place both my hands on the side of the car and leave them there even though the surface is too hot to touch. I won't move them until he speaks. I straighten my shoulders and toss my hair to one side. It flicks up and back in one clean motion.

I try again.

"I could walk back to the garage we passed and get the tow truck to come."

My father stands looking at the engine as though by staring hard enough the reason for its stopping will present itself. So I stare at him, will him to look at me. I begin to feel that I have drawn his attention. He starts to turn his head just as a car slows and stops behind us. My father looks right past me and watches the car, then the driver as he walks over to us.

The man is small and compact. He takes short steps, each one exactly the same length as the last. His arms hardly move at his sides. His eyes are on the car, but seem to take in the whole situation. He reminds me of a smaller version of my Uncle Raymond, who is a policeman. The man also ignores me. I lift my hands from the hot metal of the car, pat them gently on the cloth of my shorts before I look at them to see if they're burned. No one notices.

The man's body is turned sideways; blocks me from my father's view. I walk over to where my mother is. The little man turns our way, nods towards us, takes over. He notices the number of children to be accommodated, and flags down another car. He directs the rather startled driver to take the older women and most of the children to the garage half-a-mile back. My father and I and my two brothers, David and Michael, are to drive with the man in his car.

As I get into the back seat I notice how clean the car is and how it smells like pine freshener. There's a line of peaked caps along the shelf by the back window—Caterpillar, Osh Kosh B'Gosh and Carling Black Label are the ones I can read by their backward reflections in the glass. The radio is playing what my grandmother calls swing. The man, who my father is calling Reg and sir—"Yes sir, I thought to check that. No Reg, I don't think it's the carburetor."—has told us to keep the back windows up so the hats won't blow around. Between the heat, which presses around me in the dead space of the back seat, and the up-and-down flow of the music, which blends with my father's fawning and grateful voice, I feel my stomach begin to rise into my throat. I swallow quickly over and over again and try not to breathe in the heavy scent given off by the pine freshener. When I can't swallow any faster I roll down my window just as the car slows to turn into the station. I avoid looking at either the man, or my father, who turns to look at me. I slam my car door as hard as I can, walk around to my brother's door and slam it, too.

Reg makes all of the arrangements to have the car towed in. Once he starts something, he likes to see it through, he tells my father. After the car arrives and is checked, the mechanic tells Reg that the problem is a faulty gas pump.

"You knew that, didn't you, Daddy?"

I try to draw my father into the active part of this conversation. They're standing at the side of the open garage door facing each other. I'm just beside and behind my father. Reg doesn't stop talking, hasn't since he picked us up. He is telling my father about a friend of his, a taxi driver in Montreal who loves snowstorms. This friend has a box he had made especially for his taxi, with places for Thermoses, food, medical supplies, two ropes, chains, shovels and blankets. He drives around the city in the middle of blizzards looking for people to help. Snowstorms are his favourite days for driving and even if he's just finished a shift, he'll work on his own time helping stranded drivers.

"Now I'll have a story for him." Reg laughs. "You sure do have a big family. Are you Catholics?"

Reg shakes hands with my father, opens the back doors of his car and brushes out each side of the seat with his hand. He rolls up the back window. For the first time since he arrived on the scene he looks at me directly over the top of the window, his eyes moving up as the glass does, the contact cut the second the window is closed. He turns away, straightens the caps on the rear ledge, gets into his car and leaves. He gives a blast on his horn and I feel he needs to be a part of the action even as he's leaving it.

"What a horrid little man."

My mother's words come from behind my father and me. We turn together to face her; my father turns away again.

"You just be grateful he came along."

My father doesn't turn to look at her as he says this, but watches Reg's car pull out of sight on the highway. He watches him as though he's trying to place himself in that car, going where it is going. His feet have not moved, but his body is angled away from us, leaning in the direction the car is going. I turn my back on him and smile at my mother.

"Here, let me take the baby for awhile. You've got some spit-up on your shoulder. Maybe you want to wash it off and get a drink of something."

I point out to my mother where the stain is; I run my hand down her arm and squeeze her fingers. I reach to take the baby.

~

As I sit with the baby and watch the highway I'm sure that everyone is looking at us, seeing all these people together, the car in the bay, wondering and commenting on us as they whiz by. I remember how the garage mechanic stared at us, bobbing his head up and down to count as each one of us emerged from the two cars. My grandmother gives the children money. Get whatever you want, she says, which is one of the reasons why I love her so much. I sit with her now as I let the baby crawl around as much as possible. To let off some steam, I hope. Maybe he'll fall asleep in the car, if it ever gets fixed.

My parents are talking with the mechanic in his office and making phone calls. We can't hear them, only the sound of cars approaching from a distance, swooshing by in a flash of sun-on-glass. The cars leave a trail of dust, raised from the gravel shoulders of the road, which seems to take forever to settle. There's also the steady, high-pitched whir of tree frogs. The noise and the hot air seem to be attached, to belong together. The stillness at the end of each call is more an intrusion than the sound itself.

My father turns toward us. He calls to me.

"Bertha, go get Michael. He's playing too close to the road."

I get Michael and go back to sit with my grandmother. Her eyes are always on my parents as they negotiate new plans. Michael goes too close to the road again, but I choose to do nothing about it. I pretend not to see my father glare at me. I look down and concentrate on pulling up pieces of tender grass from their sockets, biting off the sweet, white ends and placing the green stems into a log-cabin pattern on a flat spot next to me. I sense, by a shift in my grandmother's body, that my father is approaching. I can feel his shadow move onto my legs. Though the shade he makes does not change the temperature on my legs, they begin to goose bump of their own accord.

"The least you can do, young lady, is help your mother unpack the car. I've arranged for rides to get us to Sauble. They'll be here in about fifteen minutes."

I place my hand over the grass structure and look sideways up at my father. I can't see his face, only the silhouetted outline of his head against the sun.

"They?"

"Raymond doesn't have a big enough car so he got Phil to come too."

"Aw Daddy. For God's sake. Two cars again. They'll think we're so... Oh, I don't know. Why couldn't you rent a big car or a trailer or something?"

"Do you realize how much all of this will cost? The car, the cottage. If it weren't for your grandmother helping us out we'd be going home right now."

"So why don't we? I didn't want to come along in the first place."

My eyes have adjusted to the sunlight and I watch his face grow quiet and tight.

"Go help your mother. Now."

~

When Uncle Raymond and my cousin Phil arrive, Raymond jokes about our misfortune and they help us divide suitcases, food boxes, the baby's playpen and our beach stuff between the two car trunks. Raymond tells us how, when he and my father were kids, their uncle used to drive the whole family to a resort, drop them off, then come back a week later to pick them up. Their dad never owned a car, refused to learn how to drive one. Every summer was the same. That's what families are for, he says. But back then they all fit into one car. They don't make cars like they used to.

Phil doesn't say a word.

"I'll ride with Uncle Raymond," I say.

~

It's late afternoon by the time we arrive at the cottage. There is lots of light, but it is late-August light and low in the sky. It does not lessen the heat. The cottage is on a stretch of beach where the buildings are set right on the sand. Some have cedar hedges and patches of sandy grass. Most are square wooden boxes that have porches descending onto packed sand paths that run directly down to the water. Ours is one of these. There's a rich, tinny smell in the air: warmth and water and earth.

The children get out of the cars and run for the water, curious about what it looks like up close, how it feels. My mother calls them back and promises we'll swim in the evening, after supper when we're more settled.

The men unload the cars. Phil and Uncle Raymond go for a fast swim, then have a beer from the cooler. The tall green bottles are wet and without labels. The labels are floating in the water made by melting ice that the children scoop out to eat and play with, the younger ones losing most of theirs to the sand. The men lean against the porch rail under the hand-carved sign:

"Happy Ours." I notice that their eyes connect over the heads of the playing children and do not seem to notice what's going on below them. I mention it to my grandmother and she tells me that it takes a great deal of practice for them to do this, and then she and my mother laugh.

When Phil and Uncle Raymond leave, they'll take my father with them back to the city. He's arranged to rent a small car until Monday, when he can pick up our station wagon at the garage. The fuel pump wasn't in stock and will be bussed from the city. It won't be installed until late Monday morning. I listen to the men through the screen door from the kitchen, where we're preparing sandwiches for them to take along in the cars. I learn that my father will drive me to work Monday morning, as was planned in the first place, drop the rental car off, catch the Greyhound bus to the garage, pick up the station wagon and drive back to Sauble Beach for the rest of his holiday. I'm only glad to hear I will be getting away from this luckless family.

~

By Sunday, the heat turns to a pre-fall coolness. The children refuse to take off their bathing suits and wear old sweaters over them. They spend their time in the water, which feels much warmer than the air, or with their arms crossed over their chests to hug the warmth to their bodies. I spread my beach towel slightly to one side of them all and press my body as close to the warmed sand as I can. I'll get a tan, come hell or high water. I watch my family from under the hollow of my arms which I cross to make a pillow for my head.

My grandmother and mother walk along the water's edge with the baby, picking up shells from the beach and pebbles from the baby's mouth where he tends to put everything he finds. My father sits in a folding, plastic lawn chair. He watches the rest of the children as they swim. His eyes never leave them. Every ten minutes his head bounces up and down several times and his lips move without noise. He is counting: one, nod, two, nod, three, nod, four…a pause as he looks around. I sit up and look, too. Nod, five, nod, six, nod, seven, nod. He doesn't count me or the baby; doesn't look away from the water.

"Why don't you swim anymore, Daddy? Grandma says you were a great swimmer when you were going out with Mommy. She says you even used to dive at Elora Gorge, right from the top cliff."

"Six," he says out loud. "Six. Where's Sandy? Can you see her? Sandy! Get over here with the rest. I can't see you over there. What did you say, Bertha?"

In the evening we play Rummoli. My grandmother has a passion for games and can be counted on to play anything we suggest. She even brings her button jar in her suitcase so we have something to bet with. As we play we match up sets of old buttons and try to sort our piles by colour, trading whites for blues, or abalone and mother-of-pearl for reds. We always do this when we use Grandma's buttons. Then we take turns asking her where each kind comes from. She always knows. And no matter how sad it makes her, someone must ask her about the tarnished brass military buttons from the jar. We children have an unspoken pact to take turns using them because we know it is an honour. We take turns with the question, too. It's my turn tonight.

"Where did these buttons come from, Grandma?"

"They were from your Uncle Charlie's uniform. They were in a pouch, in the package of effects they brought to me and your grandfather after Charlie's plane crashed when he was testing it. Whose turn is it?"

It's always the same answer. She never says more, but she never stops us from asking.

My mother spends the evening getting the baby and younger children ready for bed. My father shakes out and folds dry towels and bathing suits from the laundry basket. He sets them into neat piles, which he lines up by the door. Each pile is the same: sneakers on the bottom, the towel folded into a perfect square, the bathing suit on top of that and, finally, a ball or sand sifter or bottle of suntan lotion on the very top. Twelve piles all the same.

"Your pile is closest to the door, Bertha, so you can get it first thing in the morning. We have to leave very early."

"Come play Rummoli, Daddy. There's a space beside me. You're on holiday too, you know."

"Maybe later."

I can't remember the last time my father joined in our games. He used to say he hated gambling, even with buttons, and he said it as if he knew what he was talking about. Or so I thought. I liked to imagine he had a bad experience when he was younger and learned from it the hard way. Tonight I persist.

"Come on. Just for awhile. You never play with us."

"Bertha, I said maybe later."

Everyone is looking at me. I square my shoulders, sit up straight and tighten my buttocks on the chair. My face feels flat with heat and anger. I continue looking at my father who picks up a newspaper and sits down to read. It's the only thing he ever reads. He reads each page from top to bottom with a concentration I know he will not break to answer me.

"Whose turn is it?" my grandmother asks.

~

Monday morning my mother wakes me while it's still dark, her voice stretched and distant, but gentle. She's prepared breakfast for us; our coffee is steaming straight up into the bare bulb above the kitchen table. No one speaks; there's only the clatter of cutlery and the contented sound of coffee being drunk. My father rises and puts his mug, silverware and plate into the sink. He places his hands on my mother's shoulders, leans over and kisses her on the cheek. She turns into him to kiss him on the lips. She does this as she continues to wipe a dish. I turn my head away from them. I wonder how my mother can possibly feel affectionate when I know she was up twice with the baby, then early this morning to make our breakfast.

"I'll be back by suppertime at the latest. Ready Bertha?"

"Um. 'Bye Mom. Give the kids and Grandma a hug from me. Thanks for breakfast."

My father carries my bag out to the rented car. I watch him in the roof light. The door shuts. The blackness is absolute until my eyes adjust and notice the morning stars in the sky. There's no moon. As we drive, the time seems to move as slowly as the miles move quickly. My father is driving faster than I have ever known him to. It's not reckless, but sure and steady. I'm aware of silence, both in the car and outside of it. It's not a comfortable quiet; it's work to hold it, but it's too settled and strong to break. My eyes sting with the air from the vents and my own tired awakeness. We're going south-east and I stare at a line of light just to our left.

"Look, Daddy. Look at the sky."

He turns first to me and smiles, then to the front where I'm pointing. I don't need to point anymore. As we watch, the line of light spreads across the horizon and turns a brilliant magenta. The undersides of the clouds, which are black, outlined in shimmering grey, turn pink, then red, as the light expands and seems to force colour and texture into the sky. A ball of red rises in the centre of this and as the sky in front grows brighter, the blackness behind us becomes impenetrable. Silhouettes emerge: trees, houses, barns, cars and tractors, even a dog running down a lane. The colour behind the silhouettes becomes vibrant, shimmers. Then, the moment is gone. We do not see the shadows of things, but what they really are.

"Will you look at that! Will you just look at that. 'Red sky in the morning, sailors take warning.'"

My father pulls out his handkerchief and hands it to me. I am crying. He turns on the radio and listens to the news.

When we reach the store where I work I get out of my door, leaning in to grab my bag of clothes from the seat. My father takes a small paper sack that has been sitting on the seat under my bag. He hands it to me.

"I couldn't find the right time this weekend. Hurry up now, you're late."

I back out of the car and stand beside it. My father leans over and pulls the car door shut by the handle. From this position he smiles a sideways smile through the window and waves. As he drives away I unroll the bag and take out a blue velvet case, and open it. The watch, a fine, clear-faced nurse's watch, is gold. It has a second-hand that can time a heartbeat. It's wound and set: 8:06. I look up to see the car turn the corner. I see my father's arm resting along the windowsill of the car door, and I sense that he's looking straight ahead. As I put the watch on I notice an inscription on the back. It's done in the same fancy lettering I remember seeing on my mother's silver engagement bracelet.

To Bertha, it says. *Love, Dad. August 1968.*

I put the velvet case back into the bag. I roll the top of it down and press the edges into a crease until I can smell the brown paper, sweet and woody and sad. I look at the watch: 8:09. Late now, I still have to change from my shorts into my uniform for work. I decide to call Karen on my break to see if her father will let her spend the night at my house. We'll have frozen TV dinners and drink Coke. We have only eight more days together before I leave for nurse's training.

I look at the road again. The car is gone. There is nothing left to see. I turn away and go inside the store to work.

MERMAIDS IN HIS PALM

~

I do not like myself when I am with my father, so I do not see him often. But when he called this morning and asked me to lunch, I accepted. Partly because my mother had called earlier to say she was worried, concerned my father was unwell. But mostly because I thought they'd discovered that Gary had left me. I decided it was time to come clean, to have an adult conversation with my father: no quibbling, no nasty remarks.

I dress carefully, determined not to provoke: little make-up, muted colours, gentle lines. Then, because he is my father, and I his imperfect, intractable daughter, I loop a garish pair of naked plastic mermaids through my ears. Every time I turn my head my father will notice them brush my cheeks. And every time they touch my skin they'll warn me to be careful.

My father approaches parenting in much the same way he does lawn care: as if he's at war with a foe and with scientific determination, courage and vigilance he'll be victorious. Beat the odds. With measured, timed applications of fertilizer and attacks with poison; with daily weeding, raking, edging, trimming, cutting in one direction, then cutting again in the other, he'll tame and control the enemy. Achieve a visible peaceful perfection which everyone will praise and admire. His lawn is a uniform cushion of green, a golfer's delight, the envy of all who see it.

The main battle with my brothers has to do with LIFE. "*What* are you *doing* with your *LIFE?*" There follows advice, regimes and schedules, and fool-proof plans, most of which are never heeded, or if attempted, are accomplished inadequately. "Take control," he says, "Be the captain of your own ship."

For my sisters and me, the contest of wills first revolved around decorum and appearance. "Brush your hair. That blouse is too tight; young *ladies* don't wear red." Later on it revolved around boys, then men: what sorts were suitable, what sorts weren't. The ones we picked weren't.

I arrive at the restaurant early to watch my father's entrance. I do not want to be caught off guard. But I *am,* because my father's directing a nice-looking man, a man at ease in his body. I'm surprised, and angry, but curious, for my father has brought with him my favourite old boyfriend, Bernard Laflamme.

~

I had many boyfriends and each was a bad choice until I broke up with them, at least according to my father.

With George it's the eyes I remember, Arabic dark with lashes like the dense soft fringe of intricate carpets. His body was thick and as solid as a parent's, and just as incomprehensible. It didn't matter that when we danced his head rested neatly under my chin, that his cheek lay on my small, cotton-enveloped breast.

"Don't slouch," my father commanded. I was 5'10" and so was my father. "Don't slouch," as I stood at the mirror, hip thrust to the side, one knee bent, the other locked tight, a hand perched on a hip like a turnstile. "Be in at 11:00." I rolled my eyes and left.

He followed me out the door, onto the sidewalk. "Go and change that skirt; it's too short." Then, "You're too young," though he never said for what.

George couldn't kiss until I taught him. "Open up," I instructed. "Just relax. Don't bite me." I swept my tongue across his full spicy lips, tasted garlic for the first time. "Gently," I mumbled. I leaned over him, shoulders aching, lips becoming raw, his penis growing hard against my leg.

Once George knew how to kiss it's all he wanted to do. "Lie down," he pleaded. No more baseball games, no more trips to

Toronto Airport to watch the planes land, no more suppers and a show. "Lie down, please lie down." "No," I told him. "I'm breaking up with you. This is too intense."

"Where's George?" my father demanded. "How should I know?" I snapped back. "He's a nice boy," he whined. "That's not what you used to say. Besides, he's only nice if you like constant hard-ons."

"Wash your mouth out," he yelled, but I knew he wouldn't touch me. I had breasts; he was afraid of them.

And who cared about George? There was Mike, whose blond hair was long, his eyes an intense green. He had acne, so I closed my eyes when we kissed.

"Don't let him take off his shoes," my father ordered. "His feet smell like limburger cheese." "You're disgusting," I told my father.

"What's that smell?" my mother asked when she came into the room. "Mike was here," my father said. "Smells like cheese," my mother said. "Oh God!" I shouted and walked out of the room. "No blaspheming in my house," my father screamed after me. "Jesus H. Christ," I screamed back.

I called Mike. "Can we go out?" "Sorry," he told me, "I'm going out with Sarah Jenkins."

"Eat something," my father growled. "You're too thin." "What do you care?" I snarled back. "There are lots of fish in the sea," my mother said. "I love him," I wailed and went to my room.

Bernard Laflamme was the gentlest of my boyfriends. We talked about everything: parents, school, sex, our other girl or boy friends. We held hands, made out a little.

"He's French," my father sniffed. "What's that supposed to mean?" I asked. "I forbid you to go out with him." He jabbed his finger at me.

We deliberately broke my curfew, sat in the cemetery talking past midnight. "You're grounded," my father yelled when I came in. "Don't ever come near my daughter again," he yelled as Bernard left.

"You can't make me stay in," I screamed and slammed my bedroom door.

He couldn't, but I did stay in. Every night. I read, watched TV, talked to Bernard on the phone. I even enjoyed myself. I avoided my father. "I hate this, and I hate you," I told him if I passed him in the hallway.

Bernard and I stayed friends even after he left home for architectural school and I left for nurse's training. We stayed friends until I was ready for sex. That's when I met Gary. That's when I thought I'd become a woman.

~

When I walked down the aisle toward Gary I leaned on my father's arm, shaking. His arm was rigid, his eyes trained on the bright purple bow on the back of my sister's hat. I could smell the flowers—lilacs, my father's choice—reeking.

"You don't have to do this," my father said out loud, his voice everywhere. He didn't move his head. "You can turn around and leave."

My sister heard; I saw her hesitate. I turned to look at my father, or at his ear, which seemed grossly huge and detached from his head. I wanted to laugh "Ha!" straight into that ear. I stopped shaking, lifted my arm from his, let just my fingertips rest on the sleeve of his new grey suit. I proceeded.

When I told my parents I was going to marry Gary, my father turned his back on me and left the room. "So why *are* you marrying him?" my mother asked. "Because she's a fool, that's why," my father shouted from the other room where he had gone to read the newspaper, front to back, every word, ads included. "I'm not talking to you," I shouted back at him. "I love him, and I'm going to do it."

~

I was seventeen when I went into nurse's training. I was nineteen when I met Gary, and just beginning to rebel against the hospital routines, the dying, the repeated joke of the erect penises of the men whose backs I was told to rub. And tired of the dates with boys I'd known since high school.

Gary Eby, twenty-two. Admitted to the emergency room for a laceration to his right temple. He was drunk and had walked into a plate glass window. His hair was black and shiny as a raven's wing, his ebony eyes set in blue-white pools. His skin was olive and smooth. I wanted to touch it everywhere, feel it alive under my fingertips.

Gary looked at me, his eyes never blinking. He took the bloodied gauze from me, straightened my fingers, one by one, until my hand was opened flat. He held it in his own, made it circle the air across his chest, up and down his arms, pulling it downwards across his stomach, thighs and genitals. Except for Gary's hand holding mine, I never touched his body.

~

My father never mentioned the wedding, but he wore his certitude like a uniform. Whenever the subject of marriage came up, my sister said to me, "Remember when Dad told you to turn around on your wedding day?" If my father was in the room when she said this, and he always was, he sat straighter, tugged up his pants at the knee and crossed his leg in one swift, sure movement. He opened his eyes wide and his mouth took on a "who me?" shape.

These were my father's warnings: Gary drank (which meant too much, drinking not being a sin on its own). He was too good-looking. Gary lacked ambition.

~

On my birthday my parents came to visit. "Happy birthday," my father yelled through the screen, then turned and walked through our yard, dead-heading zinnias and cosmos, picking up leaves. My mother shrugged her shoulders. "He won't come in," she mouthed to me so Gary wouldn't hear.

My father had done this every time he came to see us since Gary got drunk at Christmas and refused to leave when I suggested it was time to go. As my mother chatted and drank the coffee I made her, my father paced beside his car. Finally he came to the door. "You ready yet?" he shouted, but it was not a question. My mother kissed me and left. When they had gone, Gary got out the rye and drank until he passed out.

~

I worked and Gary didn't. He smoked cigarettes and drank rye whiskey. He also had something going on the side with a seventeen-year-old named Colette. I wasn't supposed to know, so I pretended not to. I wasn't ready for the truth.

Our shared activities were Gary's evening lectures about all the things I'd done wrong that day, or how awful I looked, usually both. Arguing, which was constant. And having sex on Saturday night.

The lectures went like this: why didn't you pick up some cigarettes? You knew I was out. You have fat ankles. Your ears stick out when you wear your hair pulled back like that.

I screamed, broke dishes, slammed doors, but I found myself glancing into mirrors and at my reflection in windows. I began to see what Gary saw: a tall woman with thin legs, thick ankles and large ears. A woman who forgot to buy cigarettes on her way home from work.

In bed on Saturday nights I ran my hand over Gary's skin, down the entire perfect smoothness of him. I licked his eyelids, his nipples, across his stomach, along his penis.

Just once, I walked over to Gary, leaned my face right into his. "That's a god-damned lie," I hissed. He'd told me I was getting fat. I was 5'10" and 125 pounds. He lifted his cigarette, scorched my hair, took a drag and blew the smoke into my eyes.

After that I didn't go close to him, but leaned on the kitchen counter. I asked questions, one a day like vitamins: "Gary, why do you blow your nose first thing in the morning, and look in your handkerchief to see what's there?" Then: "Why do we only make love on Saturday and always on my side of the bed so I have to sleep on the wet spot?" And one time: "Is Colette good in bed?"

~

"I'm at Colette's. Don't ask me to come back because I won't. And don't try to call. Colette's number is unlisted. I took my clothes and the stereo and I'll be back later for the rest of my stuff." I listened to the recording on the answering machine over and over as though I couldn't figure out what it meant. I squeezed out a few tears before I began to laugh.

I stripped the bed, turned over the mattress and put on fresh sheets. I took Gary's pillow into the yard and shredded it, broke cigarettes in half, poured whiskey down the drain. I ate supper. I felt as though my skin had always been too tight and now it was loosened.

When I lay down on my bed I laughed some more. I knew the euphoria wouldn't last, reality would strike. When I was alone night after night. When the lawyers had to be dealt with. When I had to tell my parents. I fell asleep with my clothes on.

~

Gary had been gone for a week when my father called to take me to lunch. I had decided not to tell him or my mother Gary was gone until I felt more settled. I didn't want any lectures, any I-told-you-so's. I wanted no advice, and certainly no pity. Though today I'm ready to tell my father—want to, in fact—with Bernard present I won't.

My father concentrates on his food. "Nice earrings," Bernard says. My father rolls his eyes. "Disgusting," he says to Bernard. "They make her look cheap."

Bernard and I talk as though we've never stopped. "Do you remember Mary Jane Vogel?" he asks. "She moved to Vancouver and started a McDonald's franchise. She had twins last year."

"Seen 'Big' Jim Bender lately?" I ask. "He lost thirty pounds. His hair is long and he got one of those layered frizzy perms. Looks like a heavy metal guitarist." We laugh.

My father excuses himself to use the washroom. I glare at him. I tell Bernard I'm upset with my father for springing him on me. He tells me how he wanted to see me and called my parents' house out of habit. It was my father's idea to surprise me.

When my father returns he and Bernard talk about old buildings—Bernard is a heritage architect—about business and sports. My father tells him how the Toronto Maple Leafs are the only team worth anything, how "the frogs, no offence" are nothing. Bernard lets this go, is unperturbed, deferential, attentive. I daydream.

One time Bernard got his father's car and we drove around night-darkened streets, windows down, wind blowing through our hair. We were seventeen. We smoked cigarettes and threw the butts onto the road, watched as the sparks jumped across the black asphalt.

Bernard knew the history of the city and its buildings. We drove along Queen Street. "The whole town was built on sand," he said. "And this hotel, the Walper House, was the second hotel on this site. The first one was built by the Gaulkels. It burned to the ground."

Like a tour guide: "The original tract on which the city stands was set aside in 1784 as a reserve for Six Nations Indians. It was subdivided and sold in 1798." I leaned my head back against the seat, let the formality of his words wash over me.

When we arrived at my parents' house, he placed his hand on the back of my neck and kissed me. It was at that moment of serene contentment that I knew I was tired of Bernard.

I look at Bernard now and see again his gentleness. I hear his careful questions about my father's job, his health. I am attracted and irritated, both.

It is the attraction that washes through me. Soothes me, then makes my stomach lurch like the shift when an elevator begins to ascend. I let the feeling linger, stretch it out. I think about the possibilities. Finally I know this, have known it from the start: it is not the right time.

Bernard puts on his coat. I kiss him goodbye on the mouth, taste him, because I want this much at least. And feeling magnanimous I lean toward my father and kiss him on the cheek. I tell him I will stop by to see him and my mother on Saturday, I have something to tell them. "In private," I add, looking at Bernard who is walking away from us.

"Leave the drunkard at home," my father says. He looks at me, pale grey-blue eyes flinty and hard. He turns and nods toward Bernard, "*He* would treat you better."

Each word separates like buckshot. I wait for the pain. When it hits I want to strike back, slap him, yell at him to shut up, just for once. That I'm not interested in Bernard, who is too soft, too shadowy and blurred. I want to shout that Gary may have left me but at least he was hard-edged. That once he must have loved me. Like you, I want to scream. Like you.

My face blazes. My lips, two razors, dissect my face. I take deep breaths and sit down. My father turns his face from me. I watch him, see the straightness of his nose, the frowning scars outlining his mouth, the darkened circles like grainy wet sand under his eyes.

"Well," my father says.

He looks at me and I can see he will not acknowledge he has hurt me. I stand, and his eyes follow. I remove my earrings as he watches. "Gary left me," I say as I take my father's hand in mine. I place the shiny naked mermaids in his palm. "And I don't need these any more."

I close my father's fingers around the earrings and turn from him. I walk away.

~

This morning when my mother called she told me she was worried. Your father's getting dotty, she said. She'd noticed if she arrived home from work after he did, she would find him tending the lawn or sitting on a deck chair staring into space. This had been going on throughout the fall. Even in November, on the coldest days, he sat on the steps of the back porch waiting. She'd just figured it out, she told me. Since all of us were married or had moved away, he waited for her to come home. Only then would he enter his still and empty house.

SORROWFUL MYSTERIES

The night Robert killed himself, I woke up feeling uneasy. A pull at memory, something forgotten, a call to a friend perhaps. I used to remember the time: 3:36 or 3:47, some exact group of numbers on a digital display.

Now I say it was the middle of the night, halfway between our old life and the harder, more complicated life we were to begin in the morning. It was November, not yet frigid, but bleak and grey. This November held a tattery orange remnant of a gentle autumn.

That night I sensed that someone was watching me from outside. Our bedroom was on the second floor. I walked to the window. Of course, no one was there. The uneasiness continued as I walked through the house, checked my daughters' rooms, first Kate's, then Maggie's. They slept so peacefully. My husband, Max, slept on, too.

I tried doors to be sure they were locked. All the windows were shut. Each time I tested one, I looked to see if I could catch a glimpse of whomever it was I felt was there, rubbing the mist from my breath off the glass. I roamed the house, listened to the furnace, checked the stove, twisted faucets tightly shut. I tried to pinpoint the disturbance, couldn't, so went back to bed and fell straight to sleep.

My parents, while trying to understand Robert's suicide, told me that the night he died their dog started barking at the front window. It was sometime after three in the morning. The dog was frantic; he couldn't be calmed. They looked out but saw nothing. They, too, checked their house to be sure it was secure and went back to bed, and to sleep. It had been Robert, they felt later, come to say goodbye.

I was in the bath the next morning when the phone rang. Something compelled me to get out to answer it. Now I must always answer the phone when I am at home. I could not bear to hear the too pained, strangled voice of the newly bereaved speaking on a machine.

I was not sure it was my mother at first. "Come home," the strained voice said. "Please, come home. Your brother has taken his life." As I hung up I knew I believed my mother. Why would she lie? But I did not understand, could not comprehend, what it was she really meant. Robert had taken his life. This couldn't actually be true. "I'm coming," I had told my mother. "I'm coming right now."

~

The reasons for a suicide may remain obscure forever, but the exact cause of death is clear. Robert took clothes from his dirty clothes hamper: towels, socks, T-shirts. He dismantled his dryer hose, took wire with him. He brought a mickey of rye whiskey. He brought a glass.

He drove to the golf course (Robert was passionate about golf), wired the hose to his car exhaust pipe. He drew the open end of the hose through the hatchback which he then wired shut. He stopped up all air leaks with the dirty clothes and towels. He got into the driver's seat, turned on the ignition, poured himself a glass of rye whiskey, drank a bit (liquid courage, someone called it), then spilled the rest of his rye down the front of his sweater as he died of carbon monoxide poisoning.

We needed those details. As we struggled with what remained mysterious, with what we might never know, we were glad to know this at least: Robert died of carbon monoxide poisoning. Yes, we said, this was what happened. Our need was entirely morbid and necessary.

~

After the suicide, our father spoke of Robert with respect and deference. Robert had become a hero of sorts, a man dead before his time. As each of us struggled with how we felt about Robert's death, our father was consistent in his admiration and compassion, feelings he never demonstrated towards us, his living children.

Once I told my father I was furious with Robert for showing Kate and Maggie that suicide was an option for them. My father put his hands over his ears, "Shut up," he yelled. "I won't listen. I won't tolerate talk like that in my house." Then he asked me to leave.

When our father first found out from Dr. Zuber there was nothing to be done about his cancer, that the second course of chemotherapy had been ineffective, he was, for a time, angry about Robert's suicide, and, for the first time, refused to speak about him. If Robert's name was mentioned he left the room. Our mother told us he couldn't understand how Robert would want to give up on living when he himself would give anything for more of it. But at the end, when he became weak and sick and filled with pain, he would sometimes murmur, "This is how Robert must have felt." But our father did not give up. He was a fighter.

~

Our mother, Elizabeth, was a country girl, an adored only daughter. Her family called her "Babe." She grew up surrounded by brothers and laughter, by zinnias and gladioli, by family visits and parties at which everyone sang or played musical instruments. Our mother played piano; she and my grandmother sang.

In the summer there were horseshoes and tennis, and pickled eggs and home-brewed beer in kegs as big as a grown man. There were picnics with coleslaw, fried chicken, wilted cucumbers in vinegar, and lemon squares and cakes made with farm butter and cream and eggs with yolks the colour of tiger lilies.

In the winter there were home-made wines and liqueurs, even a clear, pale lilac wine our mother's brothers once made, with a perfume so sweet and heady and feminine the men refused to drink it. They never made it again.

Every Christmas our grandfather pretended Santa Claus wasn't coming that year, so his children may as well forget about him. They pretended to be sad and went off to bed because once they were asleep our grandfather cut three fresh tall spruce trees—tall enough to brush the ceiling—and arranged them in a corner of the living room. He set up specially constructed tables, his Christmas tables. With mirrors, cotton batting, and miniatures he created, to scale, three winter scenes: the crèche in the centre, the skating rink to one side and the homestead on the other.

Each was complete. Figure skaters cut across gleaming skate-sliced ice. Delicately carved animals paid homage to a Christ child who looked like my mother when she was a baby. The hearth flickered with firelight and shiny presents were piled into wee stockings hung on the mantle.

Our grandmother, a tiny woman with dark hair and eyes, skin the colour of walnuts, always wore an apron. When she said, "Babe," it sounded like a contented exhalation, like sweet, mulled raspberry wine. Our parents never said our names like that, though there were times when everything they felt, all their hurt and sadness, everything they would never know, could be heard when they said, "Robert."

"Robert," like a slight chill from a passing breeze, an opportunity slipped away, a pain caressed and held because who knows what would happen if it ever got away.

We knew very little about our father's childhood because he never told us about it, though once when my mother was in hospital having Sandy and I made supper with mashed potatoes, his face softened, his eyes got dreamy. "Pepper," he said, "I love pepper. Your mother only uses salt, but my mother always used pepper."

After his surgery our father began to talk.

"My mother ran a tight ship," he told me as we sat waiting for his turn for chemotherapy. "She had seven children and kept everything in order all the time. She wasn't a warm woman, but she got the job done. She was religious, churchy too, but Irish superstitious. If there was a thunderstorm at night, she came into our bedrooms with blessed candles and opened the windows as wide as they'd go. To scare the devil out, she told us, in case he came in on a lightning bolt. Imagine. She thought the devil was as real as this," and he held up a plastic cup for me to see.

"My father," he said, "now he was another piece of work altogether. He liked to show us the back of his hand, and my father liked a drink. He didn't know when to stop. If he came home from a drunk with some rye left in his bottle and passed out, my mother took it and hid it. In the morning he'd come down hungover, ready for the dog that bit him. 'Where's my bottle, Mother?' he'd say. 'Gone,' she'd reply. 'Get it,' he'd order. He'd rant and rave for awhile but he knew he was in the wrong no matter how much he wanted a drink. Then the begging started. 'Please,' he'd whine, 'please,' and he'd get down on his knees crying. 'Please. Just a drop. Have one with me,' he'd say to her. My mother would get the bottle and pour him one drink, enough to get him off to work. She'd pour one for herself, but she'd never drink it. Never. It went back in the bottle."

I told my mother this story and asked what she thought.

"He died soon after I married your father," she told me, "I didn't get to know him really. Besides, he was often sullen and mean, either drunk or hungover. I was afraid of him. He was a formidable man."

One time when my father lay on his hospital bed and we talked about Robert and his pain, all hidden and locked inside him, I asked, "Did you love your father?"

My father was quiet for a minute. "Yes, I did," he said, finally, "but I didn't like him very much."

PREMONITION QUILT

I am punctual and like my job, but this morning I had a premonition about my sister Catherine, so I've stayed home from work. I sit alone in my favourite chair by the window and look out onto the backyard. The chair's cover is a soft floral cotton, worn and thready. I rub it to see if my mother's magic will work for me. She rubs her hands up and down the arms of her chair, or if she is standing, circles the knuckle of her thumb with her finger. These are the ways she conjures her memories.

I watch the sparrows and chickadees at the bird feeder; pigeons on the hard-packed snow eat the seeds the sparrows spill out.

"She's got eyes in the back of her head, this one," my mother says of me. "Bertie can see what's coming before it even gets here." My mother is right. Sometimes I do know that something is going to happen. Maybe not exactly what, but something good or something bad. And to whom it is connected. I did warn Catherine. I never got a chance to say anything to Robert; didn't have the courage to tell him what I knew about him.

The premonitions only involve my family. I feel that disconnected fragments of their futures are being lived inside my head. I feel as if I am never alone.

The worst are the ones I write down. With Robert it went like this: about six months before Robert killed himself I was doodling on a piece of paper at work. Within an elaborate patchwork of curlicues and checkerboards I wrote: "OLDEST BOYS."

I listed names. "BOBBY ZINKEN." He'd lived two doors down from us and was an old boyfriend of Catherine's. He was the first young person I'd ever known who had died. He was killed while driving up to Grand Bend for the May 24th weekend. The sports car he was in, with three other boys, went off the road on a turn, killing them all. I'd heard that there were sleeping bags, clothes and broken beer bottles everywhere. Bobby lost one of his shoes, which was never found; I knew this because his mother kept telling me when I'd taken over ham and scalloped potatoes and some of my mother's famous brownies to help Mrs. Zinken through the funeral period. She'd also said she knew it was coming, not this in particular, but something, because Bobby'd been wild like his father, who had left the family for a drinking woman two years before Bobby's accident.

I wrote "UNCLE CHARLIE" underneath Bobby's name. He was my mother's oldest brother who'd died when his plane crashed during the war. He hadn't even made it overseas. Engine malfunction, they said when they returned his effects. My grandmother still kept the buttons from his uniform in her button box.

My mother told me another part of the story while we were doing dishes one evening. I was twenty-five and home for a visit. It was eleven years before Robert's suicide. "Your grandmother," she said, "had put a quilt on the frame—a pieced quilt—the day the telegram came about my brother, Charlie: 'We regret to inform you...'"

My mother's voice drifted away, then she snapped, "They all started that way! There was a calico girl wearing a bonnet that covered her face on each section of the quilt. Each girl held a bouquet of embroidered flowers. Nine stitches, minimum, to the inch, your grandmother'd said to me as I watched her doing the quilting. And Bertie, not one of them was out of line."

My mother stopped washing dishes and spread her fingers out to demonstrate the inch. Minute bubbles of dish soap connected her fingers to each other.

"After the telegraph messenger left, your grandmother went back to that quilt. She sat down. She rubbed her hands across the cloth, up one side, down the other. Up, over and down for about twenty minutes. I stood right beside her, but she didn't look at me. Up and down. Then she stood up and took the quilt off the frame. She folded it and put it inside an old cotton pillow case and she fastened the ends with two safety pins, one on each side. Your grandfather had come home by then. He stood with me; he didn't touch me either. All we did was watch her. Finally she walked to her cedar chest and put the quilt inside it. She closed the lid.

"Her shoulders started heaving. Then she let go with this wail. Why, I thought she was dying. When she turned to come to your grandfather her mouth was opening and closing like a fish, and she made a sound like she would never catch her breath again.

"I don't think she stopped crying for a week." My mother stopped speaking.

"Do you want these tea towels in the laundry?" I asked her, holding them up so she could see. I thought this was the end of her story. My mother didn't look at me. She looked out the window over the sink. I stood beside her and waited until she began again.

"She dragged that quilt around for thirty years; every time she moved she re-wrapped it and put it away again. After your grandfather died she went on a bus tour to Ottawa and saw Charlie's name in the Book of Remembrance in the Memorial Chamber. It's in the Peace Tower. When she got home she took the quilt out, finished it and gave it to me, told me to make sure it got some use. It's the quilt I use in the guest room now. You remember the one?"

I nodded yes.

"Thirty years," my mother said. She shook her head, looked over at me and blinked hard. "Throw those towels in the laundry, Bertie."

Robert was next on the list. He wasn't the oldest. I was. But he was the oldest boy. He wasn't dead, just vulnerable I thought when I wrote his name. Don't ask me why. The feeling was both clear and sad and I knew it was true. I wish I had never done that, written Robert's name. It made it seem so real and permanent. And I hadn't told him either. His life had become settled and whole, filled with normal things: a wife, Wendy, a mortgage, a good job. Horseshoes. Golf. Beer with friends. A new baby coming too. His first. That I'd seen danger there seemed like a betrayal.

One Sunday afternoon before Robert died we sat under our parents' patio umbrella with our other brothers and sisters. "Robert," I said, "remember when you tried to pull your toboggan between the twin cedars?" I pointed to the trees, which were larger, but still there. "It got stuck. You must have been eight, because that was the year I got that hoop skirt, remember? I wore it all the time. You didn't look back to see what was the matter. You kept pulling the rope, taking one step backwards, then going forward with all your might. Mom and I watched from the window and laughed and laughed. I told Mom I was going to get dressed and help you, but she said to let you do it by yourself."

"You pulled for fifteen minutes when we noticed the toboggan begin to turn on its side. Mom had stopped laughing. She just stood there and watched you. After five more minutes the toboggan turned completely and you pulled it through the trees. We predicted you'd look back then, but you didn't. 'Bullheaded,' Mom kept saying, 'bullheaded boy,' and she was crying when she said it."

We all laughed at the story. Robert too, of course. What I didn't say was, "Robert, I'm worried about you. I wrote your name on a list of dead people the other day. I wrote 'OLDEST BOY' beside it."

~

Maybe that's why I believed my mother right away when she called to tell me Robert had committed suicide. If Robert decided to kill himself he'd do it, take it through to the very end.

~

As I left my parents' house, after Robert's funeral, my mother handed me the box of old family photographs, and a parcel wrapped in cotton, two safety pins on the corners. I recognized the parcel right away and began to cry. My daughters, Maggie and Kate, were with me, so was Catherine. My husband, Max, was waiting in the car. Catherine asked what it was.

"Charlie's quilt," I said.

"The oldest always gets everything. Kate, does Maggie get everything at your house? Your Mom..." Catherine left off when my mother began to speak.

"You *are* the oldest Bertie, and you have daughters, not sons. You can take care of these things now." She looked straight at me.

I hesitated.

"I'll take the quilt if she doesn't want it," Catherine said and she reached out for it.

"No. No, I'll take it."

I use it, but only on occasion. It's stored in the same cupboard that holds the photographs, and the paper with Robert's name on it. Maggie and Kate take the quilt out of the cupboard every once in a while. They like the colours and the remembered drama of its arrival in our possession. It will never be my everyday quilt, but I didn't want Catherine to have it, either.

~

I have had a few good premonitions. Once when I was daydreaming at work, looking out of the window, I knew that my sister Sandy was pregnant. She was right there inside my head like a round smiling Buddha. I called her up and laughed and laughed because this was my youngest sister, the eighth of nine children. Even though there weren't too many years between us, there were all those people. It made her seem so young to me. She wasn't even a teenager yet when I had Maggie. So that's how I thought of Sandy: perpetually twelve. And she wasn't married. I told her she had better quit smoking because I had a premonition that she was pregnant. She treated it lightly, said not likely, not her. We talked about the dish pattern she was buying, piece by piece, and how it was on sale at Sears; how she wished she'd get on full-time where she worked, she could use the money.

What I hadn't known was that she'd taken a urine sample to the drugstore that morning and thought my call was the result. I guess you could say it was. Anyway, she moved in with her boyfriend and their son was born last fall. They got married this past summer.

~

This time the premonition has to do with my sister Catherine. It isn't because of something I wrote, but because of what I heard on the radio.

I left for my run at dawn. Max and the girls were asleep. I like to run in the early morning because of the quiet. Especially in the winter. When I got home I flicked the radio on. The announcer said a leg had been found, wrapped in a green garbage bag. An early morning jogger had found it on the sidewalk about a block from Catherine's house. The police believed it was a woman's leg, but would not release any more details.

I snapped the radio off and went upstairs to wake the girls for school. As I entered their room I caught my breath and sank to the edge of Maggie's bed. Only one of Maggie's legs was showing, the rest of her body and her head completely shrouded in Charlie's quilt. I sat and watched the fabric rise and fall with her breathing. I traced one of the embroidered flowers with my fingertip.

The sun was peeking through a crack in the blind. It caught on the fine reddish hairs on Maggie's leg, made them shine like polished copper. It highlighted a scar that ran along her kneecap, a miniature of one Catherine got one time when I'd pushed her and she'd fallen on a broken pop bottle. Catherine's cut had healed badly. Her scar had become thick and twisted. Keloid the doctor'd called it. I wondered if the leg they had found was Catherine's.

I moved my finger to trace Maggie's scar, pulled my hand back and rubbed the quilt instead. Up and down. I knew then that the severed leg wasn't Catherine's. But I also knew that something was going to happen to her because I wasn't alone inside my head. Catherine was there, a vague but distressed image speeding through my consciousness, holding some truth about her life that I wasn't able to bring into focus.

I pulled the quilt down to cover Maggie's leg and left her sleeping. I called Catherine at home. I didn't tell her about the leg; instead, I told her to take good care of herself, not do anything crazy as I'd had a premonition about her and I was worried. She told me she didn't believe that stuff. Catherine seldom took counsel from anyone, and certainly not from me. At least not since we were kids and she had to.

I heard Catherine take a drag from a cigarette and blow the smoke across the receiver. She said she was glad I'd called, she was just going to call me. She asked if I would look after her house for her while she was in Florida with Mom and Dad, our sister Margaret and Margaret's husband, Bill. They were to have a month in a condominium in Clearwater. They were borrowing Bill's brother's car, you know, Larry Richardson, the one who moved down there three years ago? She said she couldn't wait to do some driving into the Everglades, get onto some of those back roads and see what the country was really like. See the real Florida. I said sure, of course I'd look after her place; leave me the key before you go, and don't go getting into any trouble.

It is almost noon and I have not moved from my chair. The sparrows are still at the feeder. The chickadees flit from the box to the trees and back again, stopping only to call to one another. The pigeons have left. I get up to make some tea, and bring it back to the chair. I try to see what it is that is going to happen to Catherine.

Catherine is sixteen months younger than me. When we were kids we fought. *Hard.* I didn't like being the oldest in the family most of the time, but I was glad that I was older than

Catherine. It gave me the only edge I had, Catherine being faster, prettier, more athletic and more aggressive. She was my father's favourite, too. But sometimes when she went crying to my mother saying, "Bertie's bossing me again," my mother shooed her away, suggesting to Catherine that she should listen to what I said, and besides, she probably deserved whatever it was that happened to her.

Sometimes she did; sometimes she didn't.

By the time we were teenagers the rivalry began to change. Then there was Bobby Zinken's death. Bobby'd been Catherine's first boyfriend. She wasn't going with him when he died, but she was upset. The night of his funeral we built a tent in the backyard using old sheets and blankets the way we had when we were kids. The air was late-spring warm and fragrant. Instead of fighting, we lay in our sleeping bags, smoked cigarettes one after the other, and talked until the birds started up in the morning. It'd be dishonest to say we didn't argue about anything that night, but we didn't argue about *everything.*

I was nineteen when I quit nurse's training and Catherine quit school. We took an apartment together. Both of us went to work in stores: I at Vogel's where I'd worked when I was in high school; Catherine at the Swiss Girl out on Forsythe Road.

Ours was a one-bedroom basement unit in a ragged sixplex out past the tracks in the west end. Some hippies from the university lived beside us. Across from us, the laundry room wafted sulphurous fumes from the drainpipe whenever the washing machines finished draining. And all winter we listened to the electric crack of the furnace motor as it started up, the pounding thrum of the blower when it pushed warm air into the vents and the pings and cracking of the metal vents as they heated and expanded, cooled and contracted.

Catherine and I lived in that apartment until I married Gary. Six months later she married Bill Jeffries without telling anyone. Pretty soon after that she divorced and married again. Then Gary left me and I met Max. I married Max and had two girls, Maggie and Kate. Kids were not for Catherine, neither was marriage. She couldn't live inside it even though she'd wanted to, so she'd divorced again and had stayed single.

Catherine bought a condominium, took vacations in Amsterdam, then Australia, finally China. Florida would be a bit of a comedown for her. I stayed married to Max, got a business degree once the girls were both in nursery school and then my job at Cantechno. That is our history, Catherine's and mine, in a nutshell.

~

I refill my tea cup, watch the snow clouds build and the light change outside my window. The birds have vanished and I feel a shift in the air from that moment of waiting for the snow to fall, to the moment when it begins. One flake swirls down, then many pile on top of one another: soft white mounds. The snow would have covered the leg if it hadn't been found this morning. I see again, in my mind, Charlie's quilt, Maggie's coppery hairs, and her scar so like Catherine's.

I realize that Catherine and I have made it through most things, so maybe, whatever is coming for her, whatever the premonition means, will work out in the end. I want to believe this. I get up from my chair and decide to forget the whole thing. It was the news story about the leg that got me thinking this way. It really has nothing to do with Catherine.

I call my office and tell them I'll be in around two, and go upstairs to get dressed. Catherine calls before I leave. She asks if I've heard about the leg.

"I heard it on the news at noon," she says. "It was just around the corner from me. It's no one I know. I called everybody to check."

"Catherine," I say in my hardest, prissiest big-sister voice, "I thought it was yours." We laugh, then, because it wasn't, and because of the voice that I still sometimes use with her. We laugh because that is the only way we can fit the violence the severed leg suggests into the normal parts of our lives.

~

It's Friday, the afternoon before Catherine is to arrive home from Florida. I have almost forgotten about the premonition. It sneaks into my thoughts some nights before I fall asleep, but there is no worry anymore. The police report that people continue to find parts of a woman's body—another leg, arms, a torso—but they haven't found the head yet. Until they do, they say, they cannot make a positive identification. No one has come forward with any information about a missing person.

I get into my car and go to Catherine's house to give it one last check. When I open the door I notice that the house smells faintly of stale cigarette smoke as it has each time I have checked it, and of the scented candles Catherine uses to mask the cigarettes. It is set and ordered in the way of houses without men and children.

I make a pot of tea and walk around touching her things: the pink satin of a pillow, the wood of a corner table she bought second-hand and refinished, the fur on a hat she brought home from Amsterdam. I lift her perfumes and soap to my nose and smell them, then my fingertips after I have set each item down.

I look out her front window to see how her world is framed, how she might see things. All I notice is that her walk needs shovelling. I go out to clear it, put birdseed in the feeder I gave her for Christmas, and bring in the garbage cans from the street where I left them for collection.

I come indoors and because I don't want to leave yet I bake a batch of ginger cookies her favourite way: crinkly and golden with a sprinkling of sugar across the top, chewy still in the centre. While I wait for them to cool I listen to the radio and doodle on the note pad by her telephone. When the cookies are ready I put them into one of Catherine's fancy tins and leave a note for her.

> Welcome home! Hope you had a good holiday.
> Call me when you get in.
>
> Bertie

I drive home slowly, the smell of ginger and molasses on my skin and in my hair. I stop at the mall to pick up some groceries, then go by my parents' house. Sandy is looking after it. Everything looks fine on the outside. I go back home and find a letter in my mailbox postmarked Clearwater. From Catherine. In it are a Polaroid photograph, a short note on one sheet of paper and a newspaper article. The article, the size of a birth announcement, says that Catherine had an accident while driving too fast on a back road near Zolfo Springs. There were four other people in the car. No one was injured, but the car was a write-off.

The photograph is blurred. This much is evident: a large brown sedan with Florida plates is upside down in the ditch beside the road. A woman, who could be Catherine, wearing beige shorts and a pink cotton top, stands on the grass beside the car. Her arms are straight down at her sides. She is not smiling. The sky is blue, cloudless. The note says:

> Dear Bertie, Max and girls;
>
> We're OK, don't worry. The car was a write-off. Larry doesn't have collision and my insurance doesn't cover me in his car. I hope I get a good tax return so I can afford to pay him back. The main thing is that Mom, Dad, Margaret and Bill are all fine. Dad was very shaken up, though; wanted to go home immediately and we had three weeks to go. I'm fine too, but I feel terrible.
>
> Repeat, we're OK. Not a scratch even. We had seatbelts on and were dangling upside down. What a mess. I'll call you when I get home to give you the details. The weather has been perfect. Isn't that the way.
>
> How do you like this picture Mom took? She says it's the camera's fault it's blurry. I think she was shaking.
>
> See you Sunday,
> Catherine
>
> P.S. Bertie, I hope this satisfies you. Don't have any more premonitions about me. PLEASE.

I put all of the pieces back together and place them in the envelope. My hands are trembling and cold. I set the letter on the table for Max to read when he gets home, and I walk upstairs to get Charlie's quilt. It is in its cotton wrapper in my linen closet.

I take the quilt to Catherine's house and place it on the bed in her spare room, I want to mark her coming home alive, to give her a present for surviving. Less generously, I want to give over the responsibility of being the oldest for a while, and perhaps the weight of these glimpses, these distorted sad previews I seem to have of our family. The gesture is unfair, of course, and vain.

I pass my hand over the quilt and wonder, just for a second, if I should pack it up and send it to the Salvation Army. But I know that I won't. What happens in families has nothing to do with quilts and doodled words on paper. It has to do with possibilities. And with all we know and say about one another, and all we know, and can't say. It has to do with what each of us keeps hidden—like the faces of the girls on the premonition quilt. This quilt is Catherine's now. I lean over and smooth it, then pat it as though it's the back of someone I'm saying goodbye to. And as I leave Catherine's house, for this one moment at least, I know that I am alone.

HOPE

Our mother was pregnant with Robert when our father surprised us and said he'd bought a house in Parkdale. It was a just-built bungalow—orangey-pink brick, picture window, concrete stoop in front, steps and a milk box out back—set in the middle of a good-sized pile of dirt. Up and down our block were four variations on our theme, all in various stages of completion.

At the boundary of Parkdale, which was then a bulldozed crater, were farmland, Cressman's Woods, railway tracks, Pioneer Village, the Grand River and Schneider's Creek. Later, as houses began to look settled, trees lining paved roads, concrete sidewalks in place, an industrial complex took over the bush and fields: Budd Automotive, Uniroyal, Custom Upholstery, General Springs. We all spent time working in one factory or another, or at Parkdale Mall which had two theatres that eventually closed during the recession, department stores that once existed only in Toronto, boutiques, and deli shops which rivalled the farmers' market for cheeses, kässler, German sausage, sauerkraut and rye bread.

When our father first took us with our grandmother to see our new house, we drove from our cramped one-bedroom apartment on a street lined with mature chestnut trees, east out of the city centre into the middle of nowhere. We drove and drove along curving pitted gravel and dirt roads past the hopeful desolation of construction. If our mother felt anything about the lack of greenery she did not voice it then, though there were times, as the size of her family grew and our father's attempt at yet another seeding of grass had failed—because he couldn't keep us off it, he said, couldn't be there every minute of the day—when our mother whispered in a low, accusing way, "Mud. I hate mud. We should have paved the whole darn yard." Then she'd say, "Mother Mary, pray for me."

"Parkdale," my grandmother snorted, "now there's a laugh," as we drove under the wooden archway which somehow divided the houses we had just passed from the exact same houses we were now passing. We turned at a street sign, a tilting creosoted four-by-four, arm pointing left and downward, with Elm Street, lots 96-125, stencilled on it. Ours was the fifth house in, number 104.

After touring the house and yard, and checking the vast hole squared off with wooden forms that was to be our neighbours', the Zinkens', house, we all met in the basement, a miracle of coolness, perfectly smoothed concrete and space. Catherine grabbed our mother's skirt, cried "Mommy," and vomited on our mother's scuffed brown oxfords.

~

By the time we gathered at our parents' house for Robert's funeral, the houses looked as if they had always been there, solid and intimate, windows open in the summer, mothers saying "shh-shh, the neighbours will hear." The trees on the boulevards were tall, a series of alternating red and green maples that shaded the front lawns of houses which had been altered to reflect their owners' taste. Some with Portuguese concrete, angels and lions out front, Virgins in grottos in the gardens, and wrought iron fences. Others "colonial" style with wagon wheels and partial split-rail fences defining flower beds. Our father had tamed the mud, his grass a perfect, thick, weedless carpet of green, always cut and edged. Always.

His flower beds, identical rectangles at the front and back corners of his lot, were filled with red and white petunias set in straight rows. Red. White. Red. Stubbornly unimaginative, frustrating, predictable.

The spring my father died I called my mother and asked her about the flower beds. Did she want some help?

"Yes," she said. "I don't have the energy this year, but next year I think I'll put down some perennials."

I called my brothers and sisters, told them each to choose a plant, a Frank memorial perennial, and we made a party of it. A planting bee. Our mother sat on the porch and watched.

"He's turning over in his grave," she said as the beds filled up.

Delphiniums, bee balm—both pink and red varieties—daisies, asters, brown-eyed Susans, portulaca, lavender, phlox. For our mother we planted zinnias and gladioli, the mixed varieties, a blaze of potential colour. For our father we dug a new bed, circular, and planted, round and round, his beloved red and white petunias. We drank beer and wine, christened the beds with champagne. "To Frank," we shouted pouring our drinks over the bed. "To Dad."

~

The summer I turned eleven, I chanced on my father, standing at the side of the house leaning on his rake, shoulders hunched and tense, jaw clenched so tight I thought his teeth might break. He appeared to be staring at the wall, but when I got close I saw he was watching the shiny metal disk at the centre of the electric meter rocket round and round and round.

"Money spinning out of my pocket," he said when I asked him what he was watching. He lifted me up. "One dollar, two dollars, ten dollars spinning right out of my pocket, Bertha. See?"

I didn't, but I did think he might cry, which frightened me, so I squirmed until he set me down.

"Go in and tell your mother to turn off the TV," he said.

Later I took Catherine to see the meter; I held her up to watch the spinning disk.

"Now go turn on the TV and see how fast it goes." She did exactly as I told her.

"This is where Daddy almost cried," I bragged to her. "I saw him."

THE SIGN OF CANCER

~

I rub my hand along the surface of the mahogany dresser. The grain is so beautiful that I think I should be able to feel its imprint on my palm. I can't, of course, but only feel a cool smoothness like that of a large, perfect eggplant. The dresser reminds me of the one that sat in my parents' furnace room for years. It was gouged and someone had painted the sides and top white. Circles of the blue paint from the girls' bedroom, the yellow-gold of the living room walls and a brilliant, shiny red that my father used to touch up our wooden wagon and sled, crossed like crazy Olympic rings over the top. This dresser is like the one my sister confessed to shitting in.

~

By the time my sister Margaret said it was probably she who'd shit in the old dresser drawer, it was at least thirty years after the fact. I wasn't prepared to believe her, though I saw no real reason not to. I guess it was the "probably" that did it. And the fact that we were all confessing things, because we were trying to figure out why Robert had committed suicide. We seemed to think that if we unearthed our own black secrets, his would become apparent, or so we hoped. Although the revelation about the dresser was a big one—for years we'd been asking the question whenever we got together—it wasn't what we were looking for.

~

The day of the confessions we were in our parents' dining room, which doubled as a family room. Catherine sat on the beige love-seat smoking king-sized, low-tar cigarettes. She had a calcium bump on her finger that was stained orange despite the low-tar cigarettes. She wore tight jeans and a peach-coloured sweater with the palest of green beads—like iridescent pearls—in four strands over her high, soft breasts. She'd had her "colours" done to see what season's shades best suited her. It turned out she was a "Spring," so she'd adapted her wardrobe and only wore pastels, which, I must admit, suited her. She always appeared happier than she said she was.

After every puff, she rolled her cigarette between her thumb and middle finger, then tapped it three times exactly on the side of the ashtray. Puff, roll, tap-tap-tap. I remember because I found myself mesmerized by the movement, but not the sound. Tap-tap-tap. It drove me crazy at the time and even now my jaw tightens as I think about it.

To the left of her in the wooden rocking chair near the double doors was Margaret. Margaret, all dark and solid with perfect eyebrows pulled together, and eyes solemn and cautious. It was sunny out, and she ran her foot along a rectangular strip of light. She moved her extended big toe around the perimeter of the spot, tracing the outline over and over again. She wore panty hose and dress pants. A run had started above her big toe and laddered its way up under the pant cuffs.

I sat at the long dining room table in the captain's chair, a third point in the triangle. I was in one of my thin phases, having lost weight because of an allergy diet I was on. My hair was short—very short. I had decided I wanted to be able to run my fingers through it and long hair didn't work for that. So I'd cut it off. I liked to start at the front of my head and rake my fingers straight back over the top, and again immediately after. Because of this, my hair was standing on end and my skin was aching at the follicles. This didn't stop me, though.

I guess we were all a bit nervous. We always were when we discussed Robert's suicide. It had taken us by surprise, challenged the way we saw one another. Even though it had happened two years before, and we didn't feel compelled to talk about it often, it was still a mystery to us. The actual facts of the way he died remained shockingly clear, but were never any help in seeking the reasons. We knew we'd never know for sure, but sometimes it took too much energy to say that. Besides we always talked too much when we were together, especially when we were in our parents' house where we had grown up.

~

I turn to the woman in the antique store. She is sitting on a maroon settee, reading a book and smoking a cigarette.

"My parents had a dresser like this one." I say this out loud. "It might have been a little taller, but it might just have seemed that way because I was a child then."

The woman, who has politely ignored me until now, turns and says, "If it's taller, it's worth more than this one. That is, if it's in any shape at all. People will pay more for the height, especially if there's carving along the front panels."

There is no price on the dresser, so I ask how much they want for it.

"This one would be about nineteen hundred dollars, but it's not for sale. We use it." She pulls open the middle drawer, and a Thermos, a dirty grey ashtray and a mug clatter to the back of the drawer. "Actually, we don't usually have furniture unless it's mantlepieces or old store fixtures."

I nod. "Thanks. See you again. I love looking at this stuff."

I push open the door onto King Street. I couldn't tell her what my sister had done, or that my parents had finally thrown their dresser out with the trash. The day they did was the day my mother discovered the completely dried out and odourless pile of feces curled neatly in the bottom drawer. She asked us all whose business it was. We all said "not mine," while trying to hold back the laughter. It was a story too good to be true.

My mother, fastidious as always, put her hand in a plastic bread bag to pick up the feces. She wrapped this in brown paper, and tied it with a string, just as she did all our garbage. We watched, and groaned and giggled. Then she washed the drawer with Javex, which left a yellow-white spot on the wood and a sharp, gagging smell in the air. No trashman was going to know this about her family, she told us.

We children hauled the drawers, while my mother and father lugged the heavy frame upstairs and outside. We put the drawers back in and set the dresser by the curb with the garbage cans. All day we waited for the garbage truck. When it arrived, we watched the men pull out the drawers and toss them into the bin. Then they lifted the frame and hoisted it into the truck. One of the men pulled the lever of the compactor down. The wood screamed for a moment as it was pressed in upon itself and against the metal of the truck. We heard a vicious crack and the whole dresser collapsed into jagged, indistinguishable pieces of wood and was lifted up and back into the bowels of the truck.

~

I walk away from the store and across the street to the fruit market to buy huge amounts of salad greens for my diet. Still. But on my walk home I feel compelled to go into the bake shop. I purchase one butter tart.

"Just one?" the clerk asks as he puts it into a white, waxed paper bag.

"Yes. Of course!" I say. I promise myself I will eat only the tart for lunch. With black coffee. Nothing else. To make up for the sugar.

When I get home, I decide not to call my mother about the dresser. As she gets older she is more tolerant of second-hand furniture, but as I was growing up she was ruthless about replacing old, hand-me-down pieces. The first replacement set was a shiny, grey tubular chrome dining room suite, with eight vinyl-covered chairs that let out audible puffs of air when we sat on them. I can't remember what became of the old one.

Our deep-seated sectional living room suite, which had been my grandmother's, gave way to a brand new colonial style couch with two matching chairs, and end tables and lamps with bases shaped like buckets and wagon wheels painted on the shades. The worn Persian rug, with its patterns like coloured dreams, made way for a braided rug that matched the "colonial" flavour of the furniture. There was neither sentiment nor irony in my mother's choices.

I do decide to call my sister Margaret, though.

"Margaret, you'll never guess what I saw this morning."

"Jeez, Bertie. Is that you? Why don't you ever say hello first? I hate it when you do that."

"OK. OK. I was in this antique store and they had a dresser like the one Mom and Dad had in the basement. Remember? The one you said you 'probably' shit in."

"Not that story again."

"No, wait, Margaret. They wanted nineteen hundred dollars for it. Get that, will you? Nineteen hundred. And Mom and Dad trashed theirs. Do you believe it!"

The phone is more quiet than I've ever heard it. My sisters and I aren't given to silences. Behind the quiet I hear an electronic hum, and voices both faint and clear.

"Margaret, what's the matter?"

I hear a sigh. Then she begins.

"I was at the doctor's today. I had an abnormal pap smear last month, severe dysplasia they thought. But he told me today that the biopsy I had last week showed it's cancer and the cells are inside the cervix, too. Maybe in the uterus. They don't know for sure."

Each word is distinct and whole and seems detached from the one before and the one after. The word cancer is the one that registers. My first-born daughter was delivered into the sign of Cancer, so I've always tried to be positive about the word. I begin to push the hair back from my forehead as though clearing a path for my thoughts. I launch into an explanation of the strengths of those born between June 21st and July 22nd.

"Cancers are considered kind, sensitive and sympathetic. They're tough on the outside—protective, introverted—but have good imaginations. Sentimental. That's a main trait too, and family-centred. Other Cancer natives..."

I take a deep breath, prepared to go on to the celebrities born under the sign.

"Hold on, Bertie. I said I *have* cancer, not I *am* a Cancer."

Margaret's voice is at its firmest and gentlest, a tone that arrested me even when we were children because she didn't have to use it with me often. Margaret was the third-born, I the first of a sister triangle. We didn't fight as much with each other as we both did with our sister Catherine who came sixteen months after me and fourteen months before Margaret. Catherine and I have intimate, loud, competitive first-and-second-child voices for each other.

Margaret and I have less tension between us. We laugh more and touch each other when we speak. Even when we weren't supposed to talk, like at nighttime in the bed we shared as children, we whispered and drew the letters of words on each other's back. The game was to figure out what the other person had written by nodding yes or no to the letters guessed. We lay close enough for me to smell the sweetish-sour odour of her body and the milky smell of her breath.

So, when I hear the tone of Margaret's voice, even though the words don't seem to be holding in my mind, I know enough to stop babbling.

"What do we do next?" I try not to whine this.

"Not we. I," says Margaret. "Bertie, I have cancer. We do not share it. You can have it if you want it. It's yours! Or go out and get your own. I have cancer and I know what is happening next. And I'm scared shitless!"

"So am I, Margaret," I whisper.

There's a long pause and I wonder if I should hang up and try to start over.

"Bertie?"

"Yes."

"I'm having surgery next Tuesday. They want to do it as quickly as possible. They're going to cut away the cancerous part of the cervix and biopsy the uterus to see if there are any cells inside it. Will you be there when I wake up? You, and Catherine, if she can come."

"Of course. What else can I do?"

"That dresser you saw today, did they really want nineteen hundred for it?"

"Yes. Amazing, isn't it? But they weren't selling it. They use it in the store. I'll take you to see it when you get out of the hospital."

"I used to open the bottom drawer. I had to tug at it, one side at a time because the drawers were so wide. Remember? I hated Mom for having Robert, so I'd go down, open the drawer and hide in it. It was so big I could curl up in one corner. I wanted her to come down and find me there. When I realized she was never going to come find me and she would never take Robert back to the hospital, I shit in that damned thing. I felt so wicked and fine. Nineteen hundred dollars. Look, Bertie, I've got to go. I'll call you with the details about Tuesday."

~

The time between the phone call and Tuesday is filled with tension. I yell at the children constantly, then apologize and explain that I am worried about their Aunt Margaret who is sick. She doesn't look sick is what they say, being at that age when seeing is believing. They walk away from me facing ahead, but glancing out of the corners of their eyes to see how I react.

I don't.

But they're right. Cancer is like that. Sometimes you don't know it's there. You live maybe the best days—laugh, make love, go to movies, work—and then somebody tells you you're sick when you feel just fine. And you wonder how you couldn't know and when your body was going to finally give you a sign. Margaret says she feels betrayed by her body, but she's also glad they found it sooner rather than later.

~

Margaret is admitted to hospital on Monday, so in the afternoon I bring her flowers. No lilies, carnations, roses or mums, I tell the florist. Nothing funereal. The bouquet is huge and wide with summer fragrances mixed with the winter-orangey smell of freesia. When I enter the room, I notice Margaret hasn't put on her nightgown, but is still wearing her street clothes.

"What's this? No bum sticking out of a johnny shirt, no bare white legs with stubble and feet in slippers that go 'slish, slish' along the corridor? Why haven't you changed?"

Margaret arranges the flowers in a vase she brought from home—just in case—and smiles.

"It's too degrading. Once you take off your clothes, you belong here," she says. "I can wait until bedtime. The longer I feel normal, the better."

Catherine arrives with more flowers, masses of baby's breath and pink rosebuds the exact shade of her blouse.

"You're not undressed."

She hugs Margaret, kisses us both.

"I had to have one last cigarette in the car before I came in. What time do the visiting hours end? I should be able to make it through until then."

We discuss the logistics of the next day. I will be there when Margaret wakes up and Catherine will come after work.

While we visit, Margaret's blood is taken, her menus are brought to be filled out and consent sheets are explained and signed. The last visitor is the anaesthetist. It turns out he's her daughter's soccer coach. She explains her fear of general anaesthetic—it's a family fear, she tells him, and Catherine and I nod—and he promises to be gentle, to use as little as possible, and to leave his mask off until she is under. He touches her arm as he leaves and I see tears come to her eyes.

~

When Margaret returns from surgery, I sit beside her bed which has its chrome-barred sides up. I watch every movement of her body between the bars. Each frame is like a separate picture which I expect to have a life of its own. As soon as her eyes open, I stand, smooth her hair back from her forehead. Her breath smells sweet and oniony.

"There's no cancer in your uterus, no stray cells and no tumours." I tell her this until I am sure she understands. "Everything is fine. Hunky-dory."

She dismisses me so she can sleep. I take the bus home, then walk to the antique store. The woman is still smoking, still looking out the window. I approach the dresser and she turns her head, blows smoke straight from her lips.

"It's not for sale. We use it here in the shop."

"I know," I say. "I was wondering if I could look in the bottom drawer?"

She shrugs and nods and turns back to the window.

I slide the drawer open, half expecting to have to pull one side at a time. The brass handles are smooth and cold. Their span is wide, but the drawer slides open evenly and quietly. A tinny, dark smell of old cigarette butts rises and I remember the dirty ashtray in the drawer above. I wanted a softer smell, more like lemon and wood chips, or the smell of my sister's breath.

I search the drawer with my eyes, then squat down to see it better. I look for a slight indentation, like those found on old mattresses, about the size of a child's body. Or even a small one where a shoulder might have rested. Then I look for a discolouration or a yellowy-white spot that could have been bleached clean by Javex. There is nothing that looks familiar. I close the drawer slowly and stand up to leave.

"Thanks," I say. "Thanks a lot."

"Mmm," says the woman. She lights another cigarette as I leave.

I walk to the bakery.

"Six butter tarts," I tell the young man. "Put them in a box please; I want to wrap them for a present."

As I walk home I make my plan: six butter tarts, a Thermos of good French roast coffee—the hospital stuff is terrible—and I'll buy some cognac at the liquor store on my way to visit Margaret. She'll be starving by tomorrow. I'll go in the evening and bring candles, real china for the tarts, cloth napkins and two brandy snifters. And when it is time to whisper, maybe I'll even draw letters on her back.

POMEGRANATES

Before Robert killed himself there were no signs that made us think he was in trouble. If he was sad, in despair, he was very good at hiding it. After he died, everything became a sign. We had endless conversations: maybe it was the time he got so drunk at New Year's, remember? Maybe he wanted to tell us something. Maybe it started when he got the motorcycle. Remember what a self-destructive maniac he was when he drove it, always getting tickets? Maybe, maybe, maybe.

For the first two years after the suicide our father kept a shrine to Robert on the dining room sideboard: the signed bible in a wooden box, praying hands carved into the top—we had been given it by the men and women Robert worked with (they, too, had been caught off guard, wondered just how this could have happened to Robert, who was a good friend, a steady worker, an advocate for them all; how they hadn't noticed anything amiss)—laid at an angle before Robert's wedding photograph. Prayer cards fanned out like playing cards around the bible. Two pink candles in gilt holders. All this arranged on a special embroidered cloth our father bought for this reason.

During that time our mother functioned at work, but at home she retreated into herself, let things go. "I've lost my touch, Bertie. I just can't do it any more." No cooking or cleaning. No parties or special meals.

Our father learned to cook and clean, but he never made a meal for anyone but our mother and himself. If there was to be a family meal we made the arrangements, brought something with us, or came ahead to prepare, using our mother's dishes, her aprons, her recipes.

When she wasn't at work our mother often drifted from window to window, stood by them for hours looking out. If we were there she spoke to us from them. Sometimes she placed her hand against a cool pane; sometimes she pressed her lips against the glass, their shape revealed in the steam left by her breath.

On the first Sunday after the second anniversary of Robert's death, our father went to the cemetery where he spent a part of every Sunday just after mass, rain or snow or shine. Our mother called us all to come home. She was cooking a meal, be there at six.

When we arrived, the house was filled with food smells, meat roasting, our favourite cinnamon rolls cooling on wire racks on the counter. And we noticed the shrine had been dismantled, in its place a congregation of pictures of grandchildren.

"Time for the living, Frank," she said when our father protested. "We can't bring him back, and we can't beat ourselves up with blame anymore. I love him as much as you, but it's time."

~

The morning was summer perfect, the air still cool from the night. Verdant leaves shimmered against an azure sky impossibly true it was so unblemished. Each plant radiated its particular smell: the cedar hedge sweet and warm and spicy. The pine beside the steps so fresh and gentle. My mother's late roses with petals like the skin on my grandmother's hands, their scent so like hers, too. Rich and musty and dear.

I was having coffee on my parents' deck, waiting to drive my father to chemotherapy. As I looked at my father's newly cut grass, his patriotic petunias in two colours, red and white, lined like soldiers in weedless rectangular beds, his bushes and hedges trimmed to within an inch of their lives, I remembered another August morning.

We took our coffee onto the back steps (decks were not yet in vogue). The air was crystalline, warm and still, and we listened as birds talked wildly and fiercely in the trees near us. My mother ironed a work shirt for my father in the dining room behind us.

My father sat bare shouldered below me on the steps. I traced the smooth craters of old scars, noticed he had a single blackened pore on his shoulder. My father had acne when he was young, on his face, but most particularly on his back. I inherited this from him, but not nearly so badly as his. Even as an adult, my father had trouble with his skin. I leaned forward, my knees touching his cool shoulders, and squeezed out the blackhead, then got a wash cloth covered with my cleansing astringent and washed his back with it. We didn't speak.

Years later, after Gary left me for Colette, and I had been married to Max for just a year, Max came into the bathroom after my shower and stood behind me kissing my shoulders and neck. "I'm inhaling you," he told me. Then he stopped and brushed his hands across my skin. "Hold still," he said, and began to squeeze an enlarged pore on my back. It was then I knew exactly how familiar and intimate we had become.

~

During that summer, I turned thirteen and my father helped me get my first part-time job. I left the homey world of my mother and my sisters and brothers to embrace his world.

On the mornings I worked, I got up early to catch a ride with my father. My mother made us coffee, black and bitter, into which I put spoonfuls of sugar. She made us toast, stacks of it, and we dunked it in our coffee, melted butter rising to the surface, slick and colourful, a rainbow of glistening fat.

We said very little, but when we spoke it was the important news of the business world we shared: customers and selling, which salesman had talked himself into the most shelf space in the best spot, the specials that generated so much work for so little profit. And we discussed cars, for ours was always on the brink of disrepair. If I was going to learn how to drive a car one day, I had to know how to fix it, my father told me.

I listened, followed him when he went and lifted the hood, learned how to check oil, clean carburetors, replace a filter, do the plugs, keep a book with details of oil checks, mileage, tire rotation. My mother drifted back and forth between us and the kitchen counter: more toast, fresh coffee, sandwiches wrapped in wax paper and cookies in brown bags, softened and creased like aging skin, used over and over and over again.

~

As I waited to take my father to the hospital, I remembered how, for one summer, I loved him completely and without prejudice.

My father came onto the deck. "Let's get this show on the road," he said. As we drove he asked to be told about his daughters. "Something I don't already know," he said. "Distract me with something about you girls and your mother."

"Pomegranates," I told him. "Pomegranates, for sure."

~

For my sisters and me, pomegranates were everything we wanted to imagine outside the boundaries of our home town. But before that they were a season, or rather a change of season, that time just at the end of August edging up to Labour Day when the Southern Ontario air begins to smell like apples.

On Labour Day we'd drive downtown to watch men in jeans or chinos, and windbreakers and caps march behind long cotton union banners painted with dribbling black letters—STEELWORKERS LOCAL 987, POSTAL WORKERS UNION, etc. It wasn't that we were strong union people; we were respectful—our father, Frank, was a union representative. But there *was* a good chance there'd be a pipe band and our father had a passion for marching music played by bagpipes. He'd close his eyes and sway back and forth, hum a nasal accompaniment to the tunes.

Our father was too young to go to war, but he joined cadets and hoped for a long one. He was eternally disappointed when the war ended and he was still only seventeen. He would have loved to have marched behind the pipes. We'd imagine him as he would have been, striding, erect and straight, his eyes half-closed, head tilted ever so slightly to the side, exactly the way he held it when he danced waltzes and polkas with our mother.

~

It is late August and we don't want the holidays to end. We tell summer stories over and over: the time Margaret threw up four times in the hour-long drive to that dingy cottage at Puslich Lake. Or the time David got lost in the rows of Mr. Weber's corn field. David was little then; the straight green corn rose above his head, the rows forming an impossible maze. "I wasn't lost," he yelled when we found him, but he burst into tears. It made us laugh, partly with relief at finding him before we needed to tell our mother we had lost him, and partly at David's need to be perfect.

David is golden, blessed with our father's favour. His hair is like cornsilk, his body like that of a child Adonis. He calls himself, "David, The Great"; he writes it on his assignments and tests at school.

We tell about the times we went on picnics to B.A.B.—Bare Ass Beach—though we didn't tell our mother that was where we were going. (She is old, we think, at least thirty-three by our calculations, and won't understand. And she is pregnant again and tired and just happy we're outside, not getting in her hair.) "We're going on a picnic," we told her, and she said, "All right."

We made peanut butter sandwiches on fleshy white bread and took bags of whatever fresh fruit was lying around swarmed by intoxicated fruit flies—juicy red-veined peaches, tiny purple plums with flesh the colour of jade, the last of the summer's bing cherries.

We hiked across Shantz's field next to the car dump to Schneider's Creek just where it deepened and made a bend. The grass had worn away from the bank, which was sandy and sun-warmed. Trees leaned over the water, shading some sections, but there were places where sunlight drove straight down and displayed a dazzle of underwater life: swaying glittery weeds, spiny-backed sunfish and wee bass glinting stiletto-like, then disappearing. There were crayfish, exotic and dangerous we thought, and rocks that could hold precious metals. The sand was the colour of buckwheat honey.

We never did bare our bottoms, being much too shy and modest. Our white cotton panties threatened to fall off whenever we stood up in the water, or filled like balloons when we jumped into the deep pools. We girls swam bare-chested, though, and no one ever told.

Only the Zacks boys were known to swim buck-naked. They had blond hair, thick and unruly. They liked to fight and were known to get the strap from our principal, Sister Beverly. They hit home runs in baseball, played hockey on school nights instead of doing homework. They were small, perfectly proportioned, gloriously handsome. Their only sister, Cynthia, had long curled blonde hair held back with ribbons. She was tough and pampered and protected, and like us she swam clothed.

As soon as we finish telling the summer stories we feel their loss. So we talk about autumn and the possibility of new shoes for school. Of socks and sweaters from the Eaton's catalogue delivered right to our door along with a new stock of canning sealers for spiced pears, apple sauce, bread and butter and dill pickles and sweet chili relish. We get out last year's notebooks and smooth the cool paper with our sweaty palms, find pencil stubs, bits of erasers, broken pieces of crayons. We play school on our front porch where the sharp smell of warm, dilled vinegar wafts through the screen door. The designated teacher says, "Spell dog. Spell friend. Spell aluminum. Spell arithmetic. Stop talking."

Then there is a string of days when we must wear sweaters in the morning and evening. This is the shift, the magical time when our mother buys the first pomegranates, the exotic fruit of the season's change, the desired fruit, the envied treat of the autumn school yard.

Pomegranates last as long as the leaves stay on the trees, until the last fruits are placed on the reduced shelf, their skins as dry as old leather gloves, forsaken for the slick sweet pulp of winter's first tangerines.

Pomegranates come in thick cardboard boxes, each cradled in its own imprint, on green pressed-paper dividers. Each fruit is wrapped like a gift in tissue, green or pink. Its colour is brilliant red spreading to dusty rose and paler pinks, sometimes incorporating a blush of apricot.

The fruit is never perfectly round, but round enough, and while fresh the pistil still resembles the flower it once was. We wonder where they come from—Greece, Egypt, Lebanon—somewhere warm all the time, somewhere near deserts or salt water seas. Do they come on boats or airplanes? Who has touched them before us? What stories can they tell?

Some stories we already know. Once, at an agricultural fair, there was a bonsai pomegranate tree with miniature waxy leaves and tiny dark red fruit the size of thimbles on display. It had been grown by a woman from Greece with shiny black hair who was sixty but looked much younger except for a dark mustache over her upper lip and two wild hairs on her chin.

This was her last exhibit, she told us at the tea and baked goods table. She had many plants, but this was her favourite. Her husband was dying of heart disease; he needed a new heart. He was weak and terribly sick. "Some people, when they are dying, go all soft," she told us, "but not my husband. He has become hard. He has said he does not like my plants, get rid of them." She swept her arm across the table, grazed the cups, the sugar bowl, the cream pitcher.

"I have resisted, but my friends tell me I will be sorry if I don't give him his dying wish. So after this show I am getting rid of all my plants. To make my husband happy. I will give the pomegranate tree to my daughter. I am not sure if she will appreciate it."

During Religion class, after we learned our Catechism lesson—"Who is God?" "God is a Supreme Being." "How many persons are there in God?" "There are three persons: The Father,

The Son, and The Holy Ghost."—we learn of Aaron's holy robe, his ephod, which he wears while he serves God. The ephod is blue. Round and round the hem are sewn bells of gold next to pomegranates of midnight blue and purple and scarlet.

Miss Meagher tells us about sweet Persephone kidnapped from her mother, Demeter. On her return from the underworld, Persephone confesses she has eaten pomegranate seeds given to her by Hades, the seeds that are the symbol of marriage. So she must return to her husband for one-third of the year causing the earth to be barren while it mourns her absence.

"The pagans believed this was why they had winter," Miss Meagher sings to us, her eyebrows rising toward heaven when she says the word pagan, "but we know better, don't we, ladies and gentlemen?"

"Yes, Miss Meagher," we sing back to her.

Finally there is the school yard story of the girl who has a pomegranate seed lodged in her stomach. She is in constant pain and grows thin and frail. When doctors cut her stomach open they find a pomegranate seed has sprouted and a tree is growing in her gut. Tree roots are embedded in her flesh and draw nutrients from her body. The surgeons can't remove the tree as the roots have grown into vital organs. They sew her up. She dies soon after. Her name is Melody or Timpani, something musical and sad. This story is told in every season, almost any fruit seed the culprit, and is reinforced by our father's admonishment, "Don't eat the seeds!"

At our school, Holy Cross Elementary School, pomegranates are girl food. And a mother who is courageous and smart enough to buy something different, something not likely on the grocery list with carrots and milk and hamburger and eggs, is required to obtain them for us. An adventurous person with a yen for other worlds. A woman with black hair who wears Egyptian head pins, red lipstick, Shalimar perfume, who has hidden in her underwear drawer an ornately etched silver engagement bracelet with her lover's name and her name engraved on the inside. Someone who wears a daring black crepe maternity evening dress cut low in the front and back with sequins and fringe sewn on it, and black high heels—sling backs—with toes as pointed as sharpened pencils.

A mother with nine children, five girls and four boys, some obstreperous, some obedient. Elizabeth. Our mother.

Pomegranates are frowned upon as recess snacks by the nuns, and especially by our principal, Sister Beverly, because a trip to the bathroom to wash up after the bell is necessary for all but the exceptionally tidy. Sister Beverly doesn't like children in *her* hallways after the bell for any reason whatsoever.

Leftover bits of fruit leak a startling pink over texts and workbooks and clothes. Notes are sent home with words underlined: Please refrain from sending pomegranates to school as a recess snack. They are not an appropriate fruit for children. Yours in Jesus Christ, Our Saviour, Sister Beverly, Principal. And cliques, which are also frowned upon, or so we are told, form around the pomegranate bearers as they pick the wondrously lucky recipients of the day's communion of seeds.

On a day when our mother is generous we are allowed to take a whole pomegranate. Then there is the exquisite puzzle of where to begin. Use our finger nails and open the fruit, tiny piece by tiny piece, revealing the succulent seeds encased in a brilliant yellow membrane which feels like the blistered peeling skin of the summer's worst sunburn? Or bite right into the tart leathery peel, spit it out, bite again and again until a whole section is exposed and ready for devouring?

Should the seeds be eaten one at a time? Should we gobble them, juice dribbling down our chins in blood-red rivers? Should we pull out the seeds in delicate, manageable clumps and share them with the chosen few? With Janice Snyder and her sister Sandy, Darlene Gibson and Theresa Andrews, our neighbourhood friends. Or will we share the seeds with someone entirely new, like Cynthia Zacks, or the pale angelic Randy Gallanger, who is sick with leukemia and, we have been told, will soon die. Once, we shared with Susan Lang who was the first girl to wear real nylons to school.

And oh, oh, the flavour, tart and sweet at the same time. And even with all the juice there is an astringent sensation in the mouth though it leaves no particular thirst. Each seed is like a glittering transparent jewel, pretty enough to tempt Persephone again.

We consider eating pomegranates sexy and sophisticated. We think this because boys at our school don't eat them. In fact, boys seem to think pomegranates are ridiculous. They prefer to play sports, torment each other or girls, test the boundaries of the playground, or run around doing nothing, but being very loud while doing it.

Girls stay close to the school, huddle in the corners or near the doors, play on the pavement, skipping rope, throwing a ball against the wall, playing hopscotch. Girls eat pomegranates.

There is whispering about pomegranate juice being like blood, which for years means nothing to us. When we begin to understand we use words like risqué, fast, loose, though nothing even remotely sexual is ever spoken of out loud. Girls do not *have* to talk about sex, or so we let on; sex is something we *know* about, like we know boys play baseball every spring, football every fall, hockey in the winter, and pee standing up.

So we roll the seeds around our mouths with our tongues, the flesh perfect and velvety. We spread pomegranate juice on our lips, pucker and blow Marilyn Monroe kisses into the air; we rub juice on our cheeks like blush, the school door windows acting as full length mirrors for our vamping. We'd never let a boy's lips touch our seeds, no never ever, not even if he offered to pay us a million dollars, we say, though some girls betray us, begin to waver as they get older.

Pomegranates are savoured, can take days to eat, one section at a time, the remaining sections wrapped in waxed paper and stored in the fridge. We label them: Bertha. Catherine. Margaret.

Veronica. Sandra. A printed litany of our mother's favourite names. Her girls' names. We prove her fecundity; perhaps the partially eaten pomegranates remind her of ours.

They are our ambrosia, our sensual sweet reason to welcome the return of autumn. They make our world seem richer, more exotic than any we could ever imagine before our raven-haired mother, Elizabeth, introduced us to the wonders of eating pomegranates.

~

I left my father in the reception area at the cancer clinic where he would soon be pumped full of chemicals in the hope of stopping the cancer. I knew, when I returned for him, he would be exhausted and grim. He was polite to the nurses but he did not believe in hiding how he really felt from his family. By the time he saw me all of his goodwill had been used up.

He crawled into the back of the car where he lay on the seat, a blanket wrapped around him even on that glorious warm day, a plastic bucket on the floor in case he got sick before we made it home. We did not speak.

When my father suffered he retreated deep inside his illness, angry with us all, his vibrant healthy family, for being so hopeful, and so damned happy and showy about it. For a time, during the first courses of chemo, he refused to see any us but David, who brought us messages of our father's despair and anger.

My father relented when my mother told him she would move out if he didn't grow up, didn't smarten up right away. He had a lot of love and support and if he didn't want it that was too bad for him, because she did.

He didn't talk to her for a week but he did smarten up, began to live again in the world in which we all existed. "You'll forget about me when I'm gone," he once snarled at no one in particular when we were all gathered for a Sunday supper. What we didn't say was how we sometimes wanted to forget about him, but he was doing a good job of making that just about impossible.

Passion Rose

My mother's scent was Shalimar, her lipstick Passion Rose. She used a silver compact with her first initial, "E," engraved on the top in wide and decorative script. The powder inside was called Angel Face and smelled dry, and old somehow. She kept these things in her top dresser drawer on the right-hand side. The left side held my father's ironed square handkerchiefs—white—and a small brown leather box filled with his cuff links, tie clips and several old-fashioned formal shirt buttons, also white.

My mother's jewellery box was oval and made of thin woven bamboo strips. It held her engagement bracelet, a string of pearls her mother had given her and two small Egyptian-head pins, one with blue milky glass inside the shaped frame and the other identical but pink. As we grew up, we children added to the amount of jewellery, but not to its worth. At the back of the drawer were papers: account books, a mortgage to be burned after twenty-five years, and the accumulation of the year's paid bills. There were also pamphlets with titles like "When Your Daughter Becomes A Woman" giving information about cleanliness during menstruation, and how to use sanitary napkins, but little on the reasons why menstruation happened in the first place.

On Wednesday nights, right after supper was cleared away, my mother dressed. Fresh underwear, brassiere, garter belt, stockings, full slip, skirt and blouse. I watched, brought her things, held the baby. She gave me instructions for the night, some for each of the children, some for myself.

"Bertie, hand me the blue Egyptian from my drawer. It'll go with this top."

Her top was a maternity style—the yoke squared, a creamy coloured cotton, short-sleeved and the bottom gathered with enough blue material to cover her just-starting-to-expand belly and then some. This growing baby would be her seventh of nine. My mother was dressing to go out for groceries, the only place, other than church or the neighbours, that she ever went.

"Bertie, bring my cosmetics into the bathroom while I mix up some formula for Veronica."

I'd meet my mother in the bathroom several minutes later, sit on the cold toilet seat. I'd watch. This is what she'd do: Put on powder. Tweeze a few hairs from her eyebrows, lick her finger and run it along them, comb the hairs upwards, and straighten them out with the tip of her comb. Dab some Shalimar under her earlobes, also on her neck in the soft spot above where her collarbones met and two dabs at the pulse mark on the inside of each wrist. Uncap the lipstick, stretch her mouth into a silent scream and paint redness onto her lips. Right side, top, left side, top, and a sweep along the whole of the bottom lip. It was so fast. I'd hand her one sheet of toilet paper. She'd fold it in half, press her lips onto it and hand it back to me with its intimate lined impression. I'd always sniff it, for I loved the oily, rich smell. Finally, she'd pull the bobby pins from the pin curls in her bobbed black hair and carefully comb it into place around her face.

She'd kiss me lightly on the cheek, rub the spot with her thumb to get the lipstick off.

"Bertie, put the little ones to bed soon. Catherine, Margaret and Robert can watch a little TV. Make sure everyone does homework first. We won't be long."

She and my father would leave to do the weekly shopping.

~

"Bertie, I'm going to bed now. Are you awake? You fell asleep watching that damned TV again."

Max has his head cocked around the corner of the family room door. He moves his whole body in and leans on the door frame.

"No, Max, I was just thinking. I'll be in a minute. Check the girls, will you?"

He hesitates, smiles and leaves. I hear him walk into the bathroom and lift the toilet seat. As he pees I am reminded how loud and threatening the sound of grown men urinating can be. He comes back into the room again.

"Don't be long. Don't you have a board meeting at 8:30 tomorrow?"

"Umm. I hate those early meetings. You'll have to get the girls rolling in the morning. I'll be in soon. 'Night, Max."

The news broadcast begins on the television and I realize I have been "just thinking" for some time. I was watching a show where two single mothers live with their daughters. They seem to talk to each other all the time and I was trying to recall my mother's voice: conversations, stories, laughter, even yelling. What I do hear are mutterings, snatches of prayers—"Mother Mary, pray for me." There is also the sound of my name as it began a sentence, as my mother dressed to go out. "Bertie, bring me… Bertie, would you please…?" And the sound of my mother smoking a cigarette outside on a hot summer day.

I stand up to turn off the television. Max is probably asleep already, always falling asleep the moment his head hits the pillow. As I reach for the knob, David Martin, the broadcaster, begins an eyewitness profile.

"Today our city witnessed a tragic event. Francine Warner, mother to Amelia, three, and Ruth, eighteen months, was charged with murdering her young daughters."

I sit down again on the sofa.

David Martin's voice is deep and smooth. Smart. His mouth is thin-lipped with judgement. He stands in front of a ranch-style house on a wide lawn vibrant with spring green. Around the house are sculpted flowerbeds: clumps of daffodils and narcissus between multi-coloured tulips. Crinkled, not-quite-umbrellaed leaves of rhubarb are in one corner, an orange-flowered shrub, maybe quince, in another. I like this garden, search it, just as the camera shows it, for clues.

A photograph is superimposed over the flowering shrub. Two girls sitting, both brown-eyed, dark-haired. Amelia's hand, pudgy still with baby fat, is on Ruth's leg. Ruth leans back into her older sister, looks up and sideways to see her rather than the camera. I lean forward, closer to the television, to see this photo better. I almost reach out to take it in my hands. There is no photo of Francine, though.

David Martin appears, full face.

"Our in-depth report will take you through the bizarre events that led to these untimely deaths. First, here are some background details. Francine Warner is the wife of Douglas Warner, president of Warner Electronics. He refused to be interviewed for this broadcast. Amelia and Ruth were their only children. Mrs. Warner works at the city solicitor's office. For the past week she has been on a medical leave of absence."

I wonder where David Martin gets this information. Who he speaks to. Who is willing to say that Francine is this or that. This is what he says Francine Warner did:

- gave the children anti-car sickness medicine, which made them fall asleep;
- dressed them in their best dresses (I wonder if she bathed them first, brushed the downy hair at the napes of their necks with her fingertips as she towelled them dry), then in sweaters she had knit;
- locked the garage door;
- put down foam rubber in the trunk of the car; covered it with a blanket;
- placed the sleeping children there, side by side;
- shut the trunk;
- started the car and went into the house to wait for her husband to return home from work.

~

"Max, look at this."

I lifted my nightgown and placed Maggie on my deflated balloon of a belly. Seven pounds, thirteen ounces. Twenty-one inches long. She had fingers like an artist's, delicate sharp fingernails too long already. Her dark hair grew right down along her forehead almost to her eyebrows. She had skin like wrinkled silk. She curled into herself, asleep.

"How did all of her ever fit inside of me?"

I touched my swollen breasts.

"These can't be mine, Max. Do you believe it?"

Blue veins flattened out like mapped rivers on a bare mountainside. Just looking at them made my milk leak, then squirt straight out, a burning softening relief. Max grabbed a water glass and tried to catch the stream of milk.

"Will you look at that. I've never seen anything like it, Bertie."

We laughed and laughed and Max touched his finger to the few drops of bluish-white milk in the glass. He licked it.

"Very sweet," he said and blushed a hot red colour.

We dressed Maggie together, taking care not to hurt her drying purplish cord, and we took her home with us. I wanted one of those babies who slept the night at six weeks. Seven weeks. Please at eight weeks. Nine. Some nights it happened and I woke up in the morning soaking wet, smelling cheesy, breasts near exploding with the pressure of milk.

"Did you hear Maggie, Max? Did she wake up at all last night?"

I ran into her room. Her body was still, head twisted, turned sideways and back. Her eyes were open and rolled upwards. She watched leaf patterns move slowly across the head of her bassinet. I laughed, wanted to call her name—Maggie—make her look at me like that.

~

"I'm tired, Max; can you get Maggie for me?"

He stumbled out of bed, changed her, had a pee holding Maggie with one hand, his penis with the other. He handed her to me and fell right back to sleep. I slept in snatches, both night and day; walked alone, Maggie strapped to my front in her carrier. She cried. I nursed her. She cried. At five o'clock, every day, I watched a rerun of *Gunsmoke* on television. Nursed Maggie. I watched the six o'clock news and waited for Max to come home from work. When he did, I cried.

"I'm so alone, Max. Do you love me?"

He looked at me and at the baby. He looked out of the window—the longest look—and back to me again.

"You know I do, Bertie. Don't you?"

"I can't stand to love her so much, Max."

I began to list "what ifs." What if I should drop her while I'm bathing her, heady from the smell of Baby's Own soap and the responding perfection of her body under my hands? Or I roll over on her when she is in bed with me? Or we get in a car accident when I take her with me to buy groceries? Or she chokes in her sleep while I am working in the garden?

"I'm so afraid, Max. What would I do if anything happened to her?"

Maggie lived. I stopped nursing her because I hated the intimacy—my arousal, her unquenchable demands on my body. Hated her crying dissatisfaction after a feeding. At least she cried less after a bottle.

Maggie gained weight, grew longer, found a routine that suited her. I adapted, found some friends, went to exercise classes, volunteered. When Maggie had bad days—teething, flu, colds—and wanted only *me* all day and all night, when I wanted to hit her or scream, I lifted her in my arms into the air. Fast. Right to the edge of harm. Brought her down to me, then, laughing. When I wanted to bite her because she had bitten me, I lifted her shirt from her belly and blew loud puffing farts into her chubbiness.

She laughed. When she awoke and cried at night, when I wished for deafness, childlessness, quiet even, I walked her in my arms to sleep. I sang:

> I gave my love a cherry that had no stone,
> I gave my love a chicken that had no bone,
> I gave my love a story that had no end,
> And I gave my love a baby that's no' cryin'.

~

When Francine Warner's husband returned from work, David Martin is telling us, his wife handed him the trunk key. Then she sat on the couch and refused to talk to him. He called a neighbour; together they opened the trunk. The girls were dead. The neighbour, Jean Marcus, is interviewed. As she speaks she begins to cry.

"They looked so perfect. They looked alive. Like they were sleeping. Francine wouldn't talk to us; she wouldn't tell us why. Doug kept asking her, but she wouldn't answer."

Jean Marcus looks straight at David Martin, not at the camera.

"Francine said, 'Call the police; I'm ready to go now.' That's all she said. 'Call the police; I'm ready to go.'" Jean looks straight into the camera. "I can't tell you any more."

~

A year after Maggie was born, I was pregnant again. I had just accepted a job offer. I worked for three months until I awoke one afternoon with my head on my desk. I apologized and quit. Maggie and Max were glad to have me home.

I gained forty-seven pounds, not all baby and not all water. Time was measured by the increasing strength of inner kicks and belly rhythms. Max, Maggie and I watched the undulations together in bed at night, their hands pressing first here, then there. People I didn't know touched my stomach, too, with their hands. They didn't ask permission. I supposed my size put my belly in the public domain. I laughed about this to friends, and about how I was afraid to ride on elevators for fear of getting stuck. My navel became a distended, darkish brown stain that hurt even to have fabric brush over it.

Kate weighed nine pounds, eleven ounces. By the time I came home from hospital I had lost only sixteen of the forty-seven pounds. Kate nursed every two hours and cried for a half-hour in between.

This is what I remember of the next two years: lying on the rug in the playroom, in the centre of a rectangle of sunshine. Following the warm rectangle with my body as it moved. Doing this every day I could manage to be at home. Doing this even when the days were cloudy. My body knew the path to follow.

"Are you all right, Mommy?"

"Yes, Maggie, Mommy's just resting. I'll get up soon. You watch Kate. Why don't you get some crackers from the box on the bottom shelf in the kitchen? You and Kate can have a tea party. That's a good girl."

There were always two wet spots on the rug on each side of the indentation where my head had been when I got up to get supper ready for Max and the girls.

"Do you love me, Max?" I asked when he came in.

Before he answered, Maggie said, "Daddy, Mommy was crying again today."

Max lifted Maggie, kissed her, set her down. He bent to touch Kate, who held onto his trouser leg. He leaned to kiss me. I turned to Maggie.

"Maggie, would you get the mail from the front hall for Daddy?"

"Are you all right, Bertie?"

Max looked straight at me, refused to look away. Maggie ran in and handed him the mail.

"We had a tea party with crackers. Daddy, let's go get you dressed."

The girls led Max away to help him change—their ritual—and left me to make supper.

I also remember this: watching television with Kate when I had the energy to get off the rug. We liked one show in particular. 3 p.m. The man with the gentle voice came in the door, put on a cardigan sweater and changed his shoes to indoor shoes. People who clean floors are special people, he once said, and wearing indoor shoes helps keep floors clean.

He also said, "Mommies and daddies have bad days, but they still love you." Also, "When mommies and daddies move to live in different houses, they may be upset with each other, but they still love you." And, "When you go on a trip on an airplane this is where the bathrooms are." Here he showed diagrams of where airplane bathrooms were, what they looked like and how they worked. I took to wearing cardigan sweaters, bought us all indoor shoes.

~

The camera zooms past David Martin to a woman in a red sweater being led from the house by two policemen and a policewoman. She holds her hands behind her back. I think I see handcuffs, see them in my mind, but they aren't visible. She ducks her head through the back door of a police car. Her hair slides forward across her face. The cameramen jostle for position, lights flash, questions are shouted. She looks straight ahead, seems not to blink her eyes. As the car begins to move forward, pressing the media people away, Francine Warner looks once to the side; David Martin's cameraman is right there.

One look: brown eyes, dark hair cut straight around just below the ears, a slash of red across the lips.

~

My mother held her compact to the light from the kitchen window. She twirled up her lipstick, put some on, snapped the compact shut and threw it and the lipstick onto the counter. She walked over to the stove where she had started a stew for supper. All of the noises she made were metallic and fast. She looked over at me at the table where I sat slicing carrots.

"Are you finished chopping those, Bertie?"

"What colour is that, Mom?"

"What?"

"Your lipstick."

"Passion Rose. Same as always."

"Oh."

My mother took the kettle from the stove, filled it with water and placed it on the burner. The handle clanked over. She snapped the control to HIGH.

"Bertie, go next door to Mrs. Snyder's for some cigarettes, will you? I'm out. Ask her if she wants to come over for coffee. Tell her I'll meet her at the picnic table. It's too hot in here."

Mrs. Snyder kept a carton of du Maurier cigarettes in her refrigerator. As I walked home I rubbed the cold cellophane on my cheek. Rubbed the smooth package all over my face, turning it over to get the freshness from the other side when the first side had been warmed by my skin. I handed her the cigarettes and gave her the message.

"Mrs. Snyder said to put the kettle on. She'll be over in a minute."

Mrs. Snyder arrived, bringing our other next-door neighbour, Mrs. Gibson. They sat at our picnic table so my mother could sit with her ear turned toward the screened window where the baby slept. They all wore shorts, and pastel coloured cotton tops with front buttons, no sleeves.

They talked. Mrs. Snyder lifted herself up somehow when she said things and her whole body weight, which was considerable, seemed to round off and settle in front of my mother after every point she made. Mrs. Gibson's laugh came up high and fast, moved into a staccato part near the end, then dropped off and left me waiting for the next one to begin. It never did. It seemed that she had that one abrupt laugh for whatever was funny and the next laugh had to wait for the next funny thing.

I sat on the grass near them. I wasn't listening to words because I was listening for a special change in voice, a sound that meant I should tune into meanings. The sound I heard in the quiet left behind Mrs. Gibson's laughter was the sound of my mother smoking.

She inhaled, a hungry way of breathing in hard that pulled her cheeks in deeply. She made a short, tight-lipped noise as though she were finishing a little kiss in the air. But wider. More brutal. Her lips parted, released the cigarette. Smoke continued to go into her mouth as she opened it to begin to exhale. I held my breath. The smoke came out in a phoosh that was like a distant, drawn-out explosion. It was the closest sound to anger that I ever heard my mother make.

I sat still through the whole cigarette, saw the smear of red lipstick on the filter, heard the kiss and the explosion five more times. Later she lit another cigarette, but before she finished the first drag, the baby woke up and my father, home from work, came around the corner to the back door. She crushed that cigarette hard into the grass without finishing it. She stood and ground it into shreds with her foot. She said goodbye to her friends and went into the house to finish making supper. I watched her through the kitchen window. She looked dead ahead, her mouth a straight thin line of red.

~

"Kate, Kate, is too late. Kate, Kate, is too late."

A breeze from the open window dried the tears that were running into my hair and ears, making them itch. I was aware of the two cold wet spots on the rug. A prickle of goose bumps ran down my legs, then straight up my back into my scalp. Maggie repeated her shrill song.

"Kate, Kate, is too late."

Kate cried for the toy that Maggie held out to her, then pulled out of her reach.

"Maggie, either let Kate have that toy or stop teasing her with it and use it yourself."

My voice was as shrill as Maggie's, but louder and serious. I lay in my spot of sunshine, turned only my head to look at

Maggie. She held my stare and with a slow deliberate movement she held the toy out to Kate again. As Kate reached for it Maggie pulled her hand away in the same controlled and exaggerated way.

I stood up in one motion, moved toward Maggie. Maggie watched me. She lowered her arm. Kate grabbed the toy and bit Maggie's hand. Hard. Maggie's eyes left mine, turned to look at her hand, just as I reached her. Lifted her off the floor with my hand. I spanked her. Six times. I counted each one out loud.

"One-two-three-four-five-six."

I didn't want to stop, so I turned to Kate and bit her until Maggie grabbed me.

"Mommy, stop. You're hurting us."

I started screaming all of the obscenities I knew. I kicked at the toys in my way, walked toward the girls, away, toward them again. I threw whatever was near me at the wall, over and over. My voice was harsh and hurting and began to croak with hoarseness. I began to cough and gag. My arms hurt.

I slowed, looking for soft toys, ones that wouldn't damage the paint. I stopped screaming, left the room and phoned Max.

"Come home right now, Max. Take a taxi. I'm leaving in the car. The girls will be alone. Now, OK?"

The girls stopped crying to watch me. They began to cry again as I walked over to them. I leaned down and put my face right up to theirs.

"Stop it, stop it, STOP IT."

It sounded like a hiss. They stopped. Maggie didn't move to wipe the fleck of spit from my mouth that had hit her on the cheek.

"Go watch TV. Maggie, take care of Kate until Daddy gets here."

I took my purse and car keys and left. The engine started immediately.

"Something works. Some god-damned thing works when I want it to."

The car smelled dirty and familiar, a way the house never smelled. The house always smelled like me.

I turned on the radio, loud, and drove. When I hit the Expressway I knew I wanted to drive for a long, long time. The car felt solid, its movements soothing. It felt as though it was going somewhere. I only had to guide it, hold my foot to the floor.

I drove until night came, until I needed gas. I stopped at a service centre, had a coffee, filled the tank and used the toilet. A child's sweater lay on the floor in the washroom. I picked it up. It was pink, a cheap synthetic pink that was Maggie's favourite colour, and one I hated. The sweater was handmade and the buttons were little plastic flamingos. There was something crusty on the collar; I picked at it with my fingernail. I caught my reflection in the mirror and dropped the sweater back onto the floor.

I ordered another coffee and bought a package of du Maurier cigarettes. I hadn't smoked for six years.

The package was smooth and I held it between my hands like a prayer book. I started to rub my palms on the smoothness, round and round, sometimes lifting an edge to touch my cheek. I tried to smell the tobacco inside. I couldn't, but I thought there was a smell that reminded me of my mother when she smoked cigarettes.

~

One time I got off the floor and called my mother on her day off. I wanted to talk to her when I knew she was alone, my father at work.

"Mom, were you ever angry? Did you ever hate being at home with all of us? Did you ever want to leave?"

"No," she said, fast and clean. "No." Again. "Bertie, I couldn't think that way. What good would it have done me? Where would I have gone with nine children?"

It wasn't really a question. Her voice held everything I remembered: patience and laughter, dignified resignation.

"How are the girls?"

"Kate's walking and drooling all over everything. Getting more teeth. She's a bit of a pill these days. Maggie is just Maggie, steady and too old for her own good. They're just fine. I'm thinking of going back to school in September, when Kate can start play group. Do some business courses. Maybe get a degree. How's Dad?"

"Fine."

We were silent, the electronic hum of the telephone between us.

"Bertie?"

"Yeah."

"I was too tired, too busy to think about anything but getting the next meal ready, getting the laundry done, you know. A business course sounds good. Is it like secretarial or different? Why don't I call you back later? I've got to go now, sweetheart. Your Dad will be home soon and I haven't started his supper."

~

I left the coffee bar and threw the cigarettes onto the dash. I turned the car back toward the city. The highway divided and became four lanes. Lighted exits to villages and developments passed into darkness. As I crested a rise a blue city-limits sign appeared. Population: 122,000. A panorama of lights spread across the valley. I pulled the car onto the wide shoulder, turned off the lights.

I got out of the car, stood leaning on the opened door. Car lights moved closer, blinding me, left me stunned and blinking. I turned and watched, saw the tail-lights disappear, watched the darkness they left behind. I turned back to watch the approaching traffic again.

I wished Max were here. I wanted the dense feel of his shoulders and the boniness of his hips. I wanted to feel his penis grow long and hard against me. I wanted him alone for awhile. No explanations, no apologies. Not yet. No children until morning.

I got into the car, closed the door and drove home. When I arrived, Max was asleep. I didn't wake him.

~

My eyes ache from tiredness and television glare. I feel weighted, unable to move. The need to sleep is immediate and commanding. I hear David Martin promise to report on further developments in the Francine Warner case tomorrow. A story of a train derailment replaces the news about the murders. It is not what I want to hear. I get up then and turn off the television.

On the way to bed I look into Maggie's and Kate's room. They sleep through every night now, and must be awakened to get ready for school in the morning. Their room smells of sneakers, shampoo, a faint chemical edge like drawing markers or lipstick. They lie still, seem not to move or make a noise. I am drawn inside the door to listen. Their breathing is slow and steady; forgiving. I want to wake them, but I don't.

I don't wake Max, either, when I come to bed. And I haven't again heard the sound of my mother's cigarettes, though I've tried to. When I was still at home I used to listen when she smoked in the evening as she ironed, when all the younger children were in bed. Or when she sat with my father to watch the late night news.

I listen even now when I visit her in her home, the house where I grew up. Perhaps the house noises are too loud. Or she feels she must be quieter, alone with my father, more contained. But I do recall that one time. The one with the women at the picnic table when I sat and listened to my mother smoke, and heard a sound like anger.

MATRIMONY

Of all the weddings in our family, Robert and Wendy's was the best. It was in June on a day with billowy clouds lodged high in a sheet of ultramarine sky that rose forever. There was the required tension: hangovers due to too much drinking at the stag, flowers that weren't quite what was ordered, the mind-numbing tedium of multiple photographs at Rockway Gardens.

David, who was best man, was in a fight after the stag and I had to pick him up at the hospital on the morning of the wedding, his foot so swollen it barely fit in his good black shoe, a clump of hair missing from the side of his scalp.

Robert was in love; we could see it. He wanted to be married. No regrets, no reservations. The mass was traditional and long, but Robert's joy was evident. He beamed at everyone, his eyes deep pools of gentle desire whenever he looked at Wendy.

The dinner was old-fashioned: a choice of roasted chicken or roast beef covered in thick brown delicious gravy. Mashed potatoes, coleslaw, pickled beets, three kinds of vegetables. And for dessert, pies made by the Catholic Women's League. Four kinds—lemon meringue, apple, raisin and rich creamy sour cherry pies made with June's first fresh cherries.

After dinner we danced, all of us, to a mix of old-time tunes, polkas and rock music. Maggie and Kate danced with their cousins, babies with their fathers, fathers with their daughters. I danced with Max, and with my sisters. I watched as Robert danced with my mother, my father with Wendy. Then they switched and my mother danced with Wendy and my father danced with Robert, waltzed him around the room, beamed pride and delight. All of us laughed and clapped, joined in the joke.

When they left the hall, Wendy threw her bouquet and Veronica caught it. (We didn't know then that Veronica had just found out she was pregnant.) Robert and Wendy drove to Toronto where they spent the night at the Airport Hotel in the honeymoon suite. They left for Portugal the next morning.

~

I knew no one who was separated or divorced until Jane Pearse's parents split up while we were in grade six. Jane's father, Raymond, ran away with the parish secretary, Christine Schreiter, who had pure black hair and wore lipstick and nail polish the colour of candy apples. Christine was twenty-two and prettier than Mrs. Pearse, whose colouring was, unfortunately my mother once said, beige, and whose breasts sagged and tummy stayed rounded and puffy from having five children in seven years.

Mrs. Pearse was left with no job, no car, five children, and a red brick bungalow with an aluminum door that had a big, sad curlicue aluminum "P" right in the centre of it.

Jane, the oldest, was quiet and small, tiny really, with pale straight-cut bangs and the Pearse nose: thin and long with a small hook that held mucous droplets in an disquieting way on cold winter days. She wasn't liked much before her father left. Afterwards she was too pathetic to be liked.

But she was holy, the holiest girl in the school, and because of that was named May Day Queen and got to carry the flower crown for the Virgin, then to hand it to the seminarian with brown skin, brown eyes and brown hair who all the girls were in love with. Sister Beverly called Jane a little bride of Christ and remarked that Jane might have a true calling, all because, we thought, her father had left her in this pitiable state of affairs.

~

Robert's wedding was as good as it got in our family. My own wedding was hellish, tense from moment my father said out loud in the church that I could turn around if I wanted to, until the very end when I practically had to carry Gary to the car while he protested that he wasn't ready to go.

"One more drink," he yelled. "One more for the road."

My father stood by the reception hall door, lips stretched straight across his face like a scar. He always said Gary was no good, a sentiment that was confirmed when Gary left me for a seventeen-year-old named Colette.

Catherine didn't tell anyone she was getting married; brought her husband home to meet the family after the fact. They were divorced sometime after Catherine threw a plate of spaghetti at his head when he came home after three days of carousing. Margaret was four months pregnant when she tied the knot; Veronica's child three before she did. Neither one stayed married very long. Sandy "lived in sin," but it lasted.

David had an at-home wedding with music so loud the neighbours complained. His bride wore white cowboy boots and a fringed dress, and left him for an older man ten years later. Michael never bothered to marry, and Simon went to the city courthouse one cold December morning, and returned there with his baby son for a custody hearing three years later.

Every one of us divorced or separated, except Robert.

HONEYMOON PANTS

Yesterday, when I heard my mother's voice, when I heard it wail, "Come home. Please, come home. Your brother has taken his life," I could only say, "I'm coming, Mommy. I'm coming right now." I believed my mother right away. That surprises me now. I think I will wonder for a long time at how quickly I believed her.

The whole family came, but everyone has gone back, for now, to their homes. I, the oldest, decided to stay the night. Now I am alone with the terrible quiet of my parents' crying as they help each other dress to go to the funeral home. My mother comes out of their bedroom in her slip, carrying two dresses on hangers.

"What do you think?" she asks. "I have to wear the one that's right. I think this one is too tight. It pulls across the bust. I wish I had something that was just right."

She holds one up to her, then the other. Before I can answer she turns to walk to the bedroom. "What do you think?" I hear her ask my father. I can barely stand to listen to her, but I force myself to hear every word. I know I am listening for hidden meaning, answers, the rhythm that will set this out of the ordinary.

I want to do something for them, for myself, too, and even for my brother. His suitcase—my sister brought it from his house—is standing beside the couch. I take out my brother's pants, which are on top. I set up the ironing board in front of the double doors that look out onto the yard. The board lets out a familiar metal shriek as it locks into place.

I fill the iron with distilled water, plug it in and set it to WOOL AND LINEN. I test the heat with a bit of spit on the end of my finger. The spit sizzles, splits into dancing droplets and disappears. I take the pants by the legs, upside down, and hold the cuffs together, then carefully place them on the board. They reach from one end to the other as did the honeymoon pants when I ironed them.

The last time I did ironing for my brother was the day before his wedding two-and-a-half years ago. He had two new pairs of cotton pants that he wanted to take on his honeymoon. I hemmed and pressed them, searing the new creases into place, the smell of hot cotton filling my nose with sweet, summer cleanness.

My brother was a big man, broad across the chest, but with a gentle stoop to his shoulders that softened his breadth and seemed to invite confidences, as if his bones were fluid and could wrap themselves around a speaker's words. He was high-waisted like my father—like me for that matter—his pants riding up proud and neat above his flat belly. Because of his upper body bigness he needed a larger size than I would have expected, and the extra length meant that a man much taller than my brother could have worn the pants.

He was in a panic because he'd left the sewing until the last minute. I was happy to have something to do to help them out then too. Marriages don't usually last until death do they part in my family; all four so far, including my own first, have ended in bitter separations and divorce. This time we were all optimistic; this one would last. Still, I couldn't help but wonder. Hemming and ironing the pants helped to ease the pre-wedding tension a bit. When I handed over the pants, he tried them on, gave a little knee-bend dip, just as my father did, as he tucked in his shirt and settled his parts. He did up the fly and patted the belt loop into place.

"Perfect," he'd said. "I hope they won't be too warm for Portugal this time of year."

I laughed and said it was either that or cut them off at the knee to make shorts. I told him the pants would be fine. Just fine for June.

I was touched by how much my brother loved his new wife, by how solemnly they said their vows directly to each other, and by how much they enjoyed their own celebrations. I danced and drank and partied, and when my brother and his wife left the hall to finish packing, I was glad I had been the one to hem and press the pants. I liked that. A part of what I had done was being placed in a suitcase to travel with them to Portugal.

This time, though, the pants are made of brown wool. They have fine creases up through the groin and marks across the thigh where they have been badly hung over a hanger. I lift them to my nose to see if they smell clean. At least they do not smell dirty. I place a moistened cloth over them, then set the hot iron onto the cloth. I am enveloped in the steam: memories of the damp-wool smells of children's mittens and leggings drying over hot air vents.

~

When I was a child the wool smell was strongest after skating at night. The snow seemed fresher then. Even when footprints had crisscrossed it over and over again I really only saw that one perfect patch in front of me as I walked. After supper, traffic slowed, people were indoors. I would watch them pantomime their evening routines through lighted night-time windows. The darkness was sound enough.

I liked to walk alone in the cold and dark, but the night that I remember most clearly, I was with my sisters and my brother. We crashed out the back door, bold brats, laughing as wildly as we could, burping out loud, snorting and making juicy farting noises through our pursed lips.

We lay down, cracking a thin crust on the glittery, blue-shadowed snow and spread our legs and arms as far as they would go. We moved them back and forth, back and forth, looking up at the hard, black sky. The few clouds seemed as close as our frozen breath, skidding past the stars. We moved our arms and legs until we weren't sure anymore where the parts of our bodies were, or whether they were attached to us or to the snow angels we were making.

When I stood, I looked down on the clean outlines, edges glowing like a black halo around the flattened, white body, and I was glad I wasn't alone. Glad just in case that angel got up and flew on its snowy wings saying, "Behold, for I am the Angel of the Lord." I didn't really believe this would happen, except at night, in the cold, in the dark. Then we pushed each other and ran across the angels, not caring if it was mean because we all did it.

We raced to the pathway that cut between our block and the next, on down to the rink at Mercer Public School. My two sisters ran ahead, and because I was the eldest I tramped more slowly with my brother Robert, who was six years younger than I and under my care. His woollen snowpants were covered with miniature snowballs that jiggled like the cotton-ball fringes on souvenir sombreros. As I walked, I clapped my mittens together and slowly tried to pull them apart. The snow embedded in the wool held the two surfaces as if they were fastened by glue. I ate the biggest bits of snow stuck to my mittens and disgorged the bits of wool left in my mouth in a stream of spit that left a minute, steaming hole in the snowbank. My brother watched and copied everything I did.

The rinks were simple affairs—flooded surfaces enclosed by two-by-sixes—but this year, Mr. Ramsey, the rink-man, had built a full-sized wooden fence around the ice with flood lights at each corner and two swinging gates for getting on and off. That night we sat on a bench outside the gates, near one of the floodlights, to put on our skates. We three girls had high, white leather skates with eyelets at the top. My brother's skates were the pre-hockey type—brown and black leather with buckles at the sides, and rough, fat yellow laces up the front. The ankles were scuffed grey.

I got my boots and shoes off, pulled on the striped, one-size tube skating socks my mother had knit and put my already cold feet into the too-solid skates. Then I took off my mittens to try to get the skate laces tied tightly enough so I wouldn't have to do it twice. Sometimes I'd have to stop skating because my feet and ankles ached from lack of support, a feeling worse than walking on stones barefoot for the first time in summer.

It was also my job to do up Robert's skates. We didn't talk; we grunted with exertion, with cold, with having to lean over our layers of winter clothes, looking like fat curled sausages before they've been cooked.

While I was holding the gate open for my brother I noticed the man. He was leaning against one of the light poles smoking a cigarette. He had no skates, and he wore a thin, short, too-tight jacket that was more like a fall windbreaker than a winter coat. Every time he lifted his hand to his mouth to take a drag from his cigarette, the jacket lifted too and bare skin showed underneath. He seemed to be trying not to watch us, as though the smoke and his frosted breath could hide the way he glanced sideways, then quickly away again. My brother called me to hold his hand so I stepped onto the ice to skate.

We skated in circles to get a feel for the ice and to size up the other kids on the rink. Robert let go of my hand to practise on his own. He skated straight from one end of the rink to the other as fast as he could, his head down, his body leaning forward, his arms flopping wildly for balance. His ankles tilted inward just barely above the surface of the ice. He skated with a complete concentration broken only by slamming into the boards at each end of the rink. His head hit with a loud thud and as his feet caught up to his head I heard two smaller thuds. He gave a quick look of surprise at the abruptness of the stop; then he whipped around and began again.

I found a clear spot to do some wobbly figure eights, and pretended I had the grace and quickness of a ballerina, moving faster and faster until I felt I was going so fast as to be in another life. Faster until my brother used my legs instead of the boards to stop and we both ended up on our bottoms on the ice. We skated a crack-the-whip with my sisters for a while and soon our feet were screaming with cold. We decided to do circuits—just a few more—before we had to go home.

Before I had even finished those rounds I knew I'd stayed too long. I couldn't feel my feet and knew my shoes were going to be frozen. Robert began to cry, wishing we lived closer to the rink. We all knew that our feet, though wanting to continue gliding, would be like cubes stumping along the snow.

As I helped Robert change from his skates, I noticed the man in the windbreaker. He was still smoking and at his feet was a pile of butts. He had dropped them while they were still burning and I noticed that the ends were brown and soggy. I finished doing up my brother's boot buckles, tied his laces together and began to look for my things under the bench. As I pulled the skates from my stiff feet, I talked to my sisters about the kids we'd seen that night.

We were in our curled-sausage position, just beginning to sit upright, when I thought I heard a sizzling in the snow. Now, I am not sure if I really heard that sound. Or the sight, as I looked over to the post, of a cigarette in the snow which gave a last glow before it went out.

I realized then that Robert had gone on ahead hoping to beat us to the path. I yelled to my sisters to hurry, and grabbed my skates, a blade in each hand, picks readied. I felt big, and worried, and the cold in me was turning to fluid sweat. Still, I couldn't seem to move fast enough. Halfway down the path, when I saw my brother's skates on the ground, I started screaming his name and had to make myself stop because I couldn't hear anything but my own voice.

When I found him he was hatless under the dense branches of the hedge that divided the path from the houses. He was silent, not moving. He didn't react until I took off my own hat and placed it on his head. He leaned forward, touched my hair and said my name almost in a whisper. He came with me too quietly, while I found our sisters who had gone down Birch Street in case he'd gone that way home. We walked home, just one block away, and I tried to piece together what had happened. Robert remained silent. Twice he said my name in the same voice as when he had touched my hair.

My mother was at the door as she always was when we got home, ready to help us get undressed, placing our mittens over the registers and our leggings over chairs near the hot-air vents. My sisters pushed through the door first and began talking all at once. They told her of the man, the lost hat, where I had found Robert. He moved directly into my mother's arms.

I stood part-way inside the door and watched my mother undo the buttons of his coat. She lifted her eyes to me while I closed the door as quietly as I could. Her eyes were brown and steady, and I had to look away. She calmed us then, and took Robert to bathe him and put him to bed. I know, now that I am a mother, that she caressed and checked every inch of his body while she soaped and rinsed him looking for sore spots and clues. She soothed him with words as warm as the water, while she gently probed his memory.

I wanted to follow them into the bathroom, to be there in the warm steam and feel my mother's hands on my skin. Instead, I finished undressing. I sat over a hot-air vent and waited for the furnace to come on to help me thaw out. My mother came out of the bedroom after settling Robert. She brought a kitchen chair over to where we were sitting. She sat down, leaned forward with her forearms resting on her legs and her hands clasped together in front.

She didn't really look at any one of us, but I felt she was trying hardest not to look at me. She asked us questions about the man. I looked at her hands, watched them clasp first one way, then the other, over and over again. I told her about the man's bare skin, the cigarettes and the too-thin jacket. There was nothing else to tell. My sisters said they hadn't even noticed him at first.

The furnace came on. The heat rose and lifted the fine ends of my hair up around my face, tickling the skin there. I pushed my hair aside roughly, not wanting that soft a feeling; I was waiting for the pain of the thawing to begin. When it began it was as bad as I had always remembered. I started to cry with the pain and my failed responsibility.

My mother looked directly at me. She opened her hands and I moved forward to accept her touch. Instead, she placed her hands on her knees and pushed herself out of the chair. She walked past me to the stairs. As I smelled the cold coming off me and the wet wool of the drying mittens, I wondered about Robert and the secret I knew he was keeping.

~

I don't do the ironing often; my husband does it for our family. I do find the rhythm of ironing soothing, though. There is something comforting about taking the wrinkles out of clothing and linen, about setting a straight tight crease down the front of a pair of pants as if the line could direct us in our lives and keep our paths true. The smell of freshly washed fabric rising from the hot iron opens my mind to thinking and remembering. Perhaps that is why I do not like to iron too often. Perhaps that is why I put the Rolling Stones on my stereo when I do have to iron, but don't want to think or remember.

It is quiet in my parents' house as I iron today. I wish for more noise, for my own house and rock music on the stereo. Instead, I moan and sigh as I run the iron along the waistband, press the flap over the zipper. These days I have come to know what moaning is.

"Have you got those pants ready yet?" my mother calls. "I have to leave now so they can dress your brother. I have to be there by two o'clock."

Robert is six years younger than I am today. I am thirty-six. Next year he will be seven years younger, and eight the following year. I never thought I'd grow older without those six years between us.

I hurry to finish. I check each crease and seam. I fold the pants over my arm and carry them to the same suitcase he took with him to Portugal. His shirt, tie, tweed jacket and underwear are already there.

I lift the pants to my cheek and rub their just-ironed warmth against my skin. The rough wool brings my cheeks alive with a prickly feeling. I whisper a wish for my brother and set the pants in place beside his shirt. And as I close the suitcase I ask the pants if they know the secrets he took with him when he died.

HOLY DAYS OF OBLIGATION

~

The litany of our names was like a chanted Gregorian evocation of the saints: "Bertie-Catherine-Margaret-Robert-David-Ronnie-Michael-Sandy-Simon." Our mother sang it all in one breath. Our father never used it. He told one or the other of us to go and find the others. "Now! Supper's ready, now!"

We took turns singing the song for our children, for nieces and nephews, for family friends, and for the new friend meeting us all for the first time, the one brought home to Christmas dinner, or to a party. Since Robert's suicide we'd stopped singing the supper song. Leaving Robert out was unthinkable. Leaving him in was a reminder of how much we'd changed, how what we believed to be permanent and true, wasn't. The empty space where Robert's name should have been held no clues to his death.

The night after Robert killed himself my father cried. It was the first time I'd heard him cry out loud and it sounded like the distant and ferocious rumble of an approaching train. It shook the floors. "It's my fault," was part of that cry. Deep. Massive with the weight and sureness of guilt and evil. "It's my fault. It's all my fault. It's my fault." I came to believe my father. I found nowhere else to place the blame that a suicide first demands.

~

I finished dressing and left for the hospital to have breakfast with my father before I went to work. It was my routine because my mother's job wasn't as flexible as mine and I liked spending this part of my day with him. On the bus I daydreamed about the domestic habits my father had. Rituals he'd shared with me. Like dunking buttered toast in coffee or polishing shoes on Sunday morning before mass.

~

There was a sureness about Sunday. I got up on time. If I was going to Communion I didn't eat, so already the morning was different. Set apart. My father told me to get all of the shoes and we'd polish them together. Even though we did this every week, he always made it seem as though this time was the first time. I spread newspapers on the dining room floor and lined up the shoes by colour and size—my father's black shoes, the older children's brown oxfords, the little ones' white shoes and the babies' soft leather booties. I don't remember my mother's Sunday shoes at all.

There was a certain way to do the shoes: brush off all the outdoor dirt with the hard bristle brush. Put a fresh layer of paper over the dirt so it didn't get into the polish. Hold the round tin in the palm of the hand and turn the metal lever on the side. The lid popped, the polish shone and smelled like wax and cleaning chemicals. Using a soft rag, rub a thin layer of polish (not too much!) onto the leather starting at the toe and moving toward the heel. Repeat from the toe down the other side. Apply the polish with a circular motion. Don't get any polish on the sole or it would mark the floor and my mother would moan, "Mother Mary, pray for me!" as she wiped it up.

Give the polish time to dry (go on to the next shoe) or else, my father said, the polish wouldn't set. I followed his rules about shoes because they seemed to matter to him. And they worked.

Rub the shoe with the buffing cloth until the leather began to glow and get warm. The smell got stronger. The smell of Sunday morning, to me. My father got out the buffing brushes. He buffed. It took muscle, he said, and he was stronger. (Once, when my father was in the hospital, I got to buff the shoes. I cried the whole time.) He brushed it until he saw his face in the leather.

Our brown oxfords were done the same way as his black shoes, except with their own rags and brushes.

We used Scuff-Kote on the white shoes, which was cheating because it wasn't real polish and was applied with a wand.

When we were finished I placed the shoes back on the paper. Then all hell broke loose as the whole family got dressed to leave for church. My father changed and washed up, slicked back his hair, and as he came out of the bathroom he tucked his shirt into his pants, gave a little knee-bend dip to get everything into place, zipped up his fly and tightened his belt. He looked at our shoes for a minute before he put on his suit coat, his shoes and went outside to start the car.

~

"I was just thinking about polishing shoes," I told my father as I took off my coat. His breakfast tray was waiting on the table. My father's face reminded me of photographs of just released prisoners-of-war: skeletal and grey, covered with a rash and stubble and on the edge of some expression if only there was enough energy. Most of his hair was gone, found in wads on his pillow one morning during a second round of chemotherapy after more tumours were found. There were a few wisps, which looked like bits of dried grass poking through the smoothness of the first winter snow.

"I'm not hungry," he said. He sat up and lifted the plastic cover off his oatmeal. He put the lid back but left his hand there covering the bowl. "Sometimes I just think of food and it makes me sick. Still I can't get it off my mind. I did eat supper last night and it stayed down." He did not look at me as he spoke, but at his hand which was bruised from the ritual blood lettings for tests. "I think I'm still full from last night." These were the things we talked about, the ways in which we measured hope.

"Shoes were Sunday," my father said to me. He looked up and right into my eyes. "But what about Holy Days of Obligation?"

~

Their favourite Holy Day is Good Friday, when they have take-out fish and chips from The Stones of Rockway Restaurant. The best in town, Frank maintains, and his family agrees. After the zealous piety of Lent—the extra masses, The Stations of the Cross, the giving up of sweets and treats—Good Friday services peak in an extreme of lengthy prayers and devotions, a long fast, a weariness at keeping vigil with Christ's suffering and death: the reception of the cross, the first fall, the meeting with His mother, Simon of Cyrene carries the cross… But combined with the feeling of hardship is the feeling of coming to the end. And Frank's yearly decision to order fish and chips fills his family with a feeling of delighted, rising happiness.

Frank takes a sheet of paper and asks each of his nine children how many pieces of fish they want, and whether they can eat a whole order of fries. "Remember how big the orders are…Michael didn't eat all of his last year, if you recall," he reminds them. There is no malice in his voice. He will order exactly what he is told. Frank's children tell him what they want and eye him warily, as though at any moment he will change back into the father they know.

Frank calls the restaurant with the order and asks how long before it will be ready. They sit and wait and wonder out loud if this is a good time to leave because if the traffic is heavy it will take fifteen minutes, but if there is no traffic (a miracle, they say) it won't take so long, and really, the waitress said it would be ready in half an hour so they may as well wait a little longer at home. And isn't it awful when they get there too soon and have to wait in line. One year, the year David broke his leg, remember, the line went all the way out the door and around the side of the building. Imagine that, someone says. This year, it's Margaret's and Sandy's turn to go with Frank; get your coats on, the wind is cold, their mother tells them. Frank slips on his jacket.

While Frank is gone they get out the paper plates, napkins, ketchup, salt and vinegar. Catherine stations herself at the window and calls, "Here comes a car," and "Nope, it's not Dad," and

"Nothing yet," and "He's coming! They're here!" David hits Michael, who howls. Simon wakes up from his nap and begins to cry. Elizabeth yells to them all to settle down and get to the table. They push and shove at the chairs; everyone wants to sit beside Frank or Sandy or Margaret who will tell them about the line-up, where they had to park, who they knew and talked to while they were waiting for the fish and chips.

Frank comes in and frowns at the noise, but doesn't comment. "Let's eat," he says as he empties the brown paper bags with dark markings where the grease has seeped through. The food has a slightly papery odour and Frank says, "Mother, you serve." She opens the boxes and oh, this one has golden brown pieces of steaming fish, and so does this one. Bertha says she hopes the numbers are right because she's starved and the next box has French fries and sure enough there is plenty to go around. "There never looks to be enough," someone laughs, and "go get the salt from the back of the stove," and "please pass the ketchup." Somehow the first mouthful goes in, the taste of fries with their quickly uncrisping texture—but no one complains—and their earthy potato tang and the spice of the ketchup, the saltiness, the zing of vinegar. And they're really too hot, but that doesn't stop anyone.

They eat faster and faster because the food tastes so good, and there might be second helpings, and because it's special. The fish is pure white inside its golden coat of batter, a marvel to look at. And it tastes sweet, not at all fishy. The batter has a doughnutty flavour, delicious, but suddenly there isn't room for another mouthful. Everyone slows down, begins to pick at their fries. "Just two more," Robert says and groans. There's lots left over, was never any need to eat so fast, and the smell begins to change. It is heavier, thick with grease and vinegar and fish. The bags are slippery as Bertha and Elizabeth fill them with garbage. "Who's going to Vigil tomorrow?" Elizabeth asks. "I'm stuffed" is all the answer she gets.

~

I rubbed the skin around my eyes with my fists, pressed it hard onto the bone. The heat and dry air in the hospital made my sinuses feel as if they would explode. Dr. Zuber came in to visit my father. He came every weekday, and even on the weekend if he was checking on an emergency patient, or attending someone who was dying. We looked forward to seeing him. When his visit was over I would leave to go to work.

He was short, with wavy mounds of unruly greying hair. Several wild thick grey hairs jutted from his eyebrows, and one or two from his ears, as well. That day we were waiting for the results of the CAT scan that would tell us how successful the chemotherapy had been.

"Sinuses sore?" he asked me, and I was not surprised that he knew what was bothering me. When he visited he leaned his hip into the foot of my father's high bed. He looked at him and asked the exact right questions: "A little pain today, Frank?" when my father had a bad night. Or "Do you need any cream for your rash?" when my father had just discovered a rash on his arm the afternoon before. Dr. Zuber told us of the latest drugs, the laser surgery a colleague had just performed on a tumour, a success with deep radiation, what could be done with machines. Every time he visited there was something new, something to make us feel optimistic.

After he asked about my sinuses, he moved to the window. He looked out and didn't turn to face us. It was a raw day, he told us. His car battery had died. It had never done that in November before. The wind was out of the north, that must be why. He had a finger that got frost bite when he was a child and it turned white on cold days.

"See," he said, and he turned and walked over to the bed to show us. "I'll be in again tomorrow," he told my father in a voice that had begun to sound as flat and hard as ice. My father didn't answer, but looked at the place where Dr. Zuber had stood by the window.

Dr. Zuber left. I watched him go and wondered about what he hadn't told us. When I turned to ask my father what he thought, I saw that he was crying. It was not like the time he cried for Robert. This time his crying had no sound. He held it in a place inside himself. "Call your mother," he told me. "I'm going home."

~

By the time we left for Robert's funeral my father had stopped crying. Both he and my mother were tight-lipped and drawn. The days before the funeral had been filled with asking ourselves why Robert had killed himself, and telling those who asked us that same question, "We don't know why."

"Do you know why?" asked Mrs. Zinken, our neighbour, when she brought us ham and scalloped potatoes and assorted squares that were bulging with marshmallows or covered in icing the savage carnival-pink of candy floss. She too had lost a son, she said, so she knew what we were going through.

"No, we don't know why," I told her as I thanked her for the food. "He must have been terribly sad," I said, and though it must have been true, it sounded trite and meaningless. "How *are* your parents?" she asked.

The cemetery was barren and tidy. There were odd bits of colour, reds and yellows mostly, where someone had stuck a bouquet of plastic flowers into a vase near a headstone. Robert's grave looked raw and tawdry. The drab brown of drying earth showed from beneath a shimmering emerald-green blanket of synthetic grass. After Robert was lowered into the grave, a melodrama of family pain began. David wanted to know why Robert hadn't talked to him, hadn't confided. He shouted this. Michael began to cry and couldn't stop. Robert's wife left to go home with her mother. Veronica said that she couldn't stop shivering and her teeth knocked together so violently that all of us could hear them. We couldn't seem to leave.

I took my mother's hand. "Let's go," I said. She walked with me to the top of a squat hill beside the path that led back to the limousines. "I have to wait for Frank," she told me. I sat on the dry, brown grass, still holding her hand. She crouched down, leaned against me. She whispered into my ear, "Bertie, what will we do?"

We waited. Then my mother let go of my hand and lay down along the edge of the hill. She set her purse on the grass, crossed her arms on her chest and began to roll. I watched her; bits of grass and twigs stuck to her coat. Her scarf came undone and flapped about her face. I set my purse on the grass beside hers and rolled. Catherine, Margaret, Veronica and Sandy came to the hill and followed us.

We didn't laugh, or even smile. Someone, Margaret, I think, said, "This is for you, Robert." Her words tumbled round and round like brittle leaves caught whirling in the wind. My father and brothers picked up our purses or turned away.

I remember each bump, each sharp, jutting stone on that solid, hard ground.

Four years later, sitting with my father during his illness, was the first November in which the possible reasons for Robert's death didn't haunt me. I had ceased to blame my father. Though he said four years ago that he was at fault, I knew he wasn't.

There was no one thing to make me understand. My father had his bits of information, his secrets about Robert and himself, just as I had mine. But neither of us had accumulated enough secrets, or guilt, to cause a death.

Robert had done what he had to do. Only he understood. That was our mystery.

THE MUSTARD JACKET

Elizabeth sits rooted to the chair in the spare bedroom where she has been sleeping since Frank went into the hospital. She is supposed to leave to pick him up, but she can't move. There's something she must remember, something nagging at her about Frank's coming home. Whatever it is, it's all mixed up with old memories. And not the ones she needs to get her out of this chair.

Elizabeth rubs her palms up and down the arms of the chair. The velveteen upholstery darkens as she rubs upward, lightens as she presses the nap down. She prints "FRANK" into the material with her finger. She starts to print her name under Frank's and realizes she won't have enough room for all of it: E-L-I-Z-A...

Elizabeth. The kids used to say, "Remember for us when Dad proposed, Mom. When he called you Elizabeth." Frank had taken the bus all the way to London, walked straight into the residence, had her buzzed down. In front of everyone, he'd knelt on the floor and said, "Elizabeth, will you marry me?" He'd waited one long, quiet minute. Stood up. He'd told her she didn't have to answer right away, but he wanted her to know he wasn't going to ask again. "You know where I live, when you're ready," he'd said. He'd kissed her and left to get the next bus home because he had to get to work yet that day.

"I was the only girl out of six kids. I was the youngest too. Nobody ever called me Elizabeth; they called me Babe. Even Frank called me Babe until the day he proposed. When he said 'Elizabeth' I didn't answer right away because I'd never heard my name out loud. I kept listening to the way it sounded inside my head. Elizabeth. Elizabeth. I guess Frank thought I was hesitating, because he barely waited a beat before he stood up, kissed me on the lips and was gone. That's when I noticed the mustard jacket."

Elizabeth brushes at the chair again, wiping out the names, and prints MUSTARD into the velveteen.

"The jacket was tailor-made, I could tell from the fit: wide across the shoulders, but no droop. Padded. It came in sharply to his waist, fitted perfectly over his hips and down to his thighs. The pants were wide in the leg and came to the narrowest cuff I'd ever seen. The pants and jacket were the colour of mustard. I was so surprised by how fast everything went, I didn't notice that suit until he walked away! Never said a word about it. I knew he'd worn it for me. He still has that jacket around here somewhere. Couldn't get into the pants if he tried."

Elizabeth pushes herself out of the chair and goes to the closet. She doesn't have to look far before she finds it. She holds up the jacket on its hanger. Frank bought a special hanger—thick-grained wood with wide, rounded ends like shoulder pads—so the jacket wouldn't get damaged or lose its shape. He treated the jacket like a treasure, hiding it where the children wouldn't get their dirty fingers on it, then forgetting where he'd put it. She told him to write down which closet he'd put it in, but he never did. When he wanted the jacket, he searched and searched. She ignored him until he called out, "Mother, where is my mustard jacket?"

She didn't mind his asking where it was, but she hated him calling her "Mother." She had enough children doing that without him doing it too. He only said it when he needed something. So she treated him the way she treated the children when they lost things. She made them go through everything they'd done on the day they last remembered having the lost article. With the kids it was an exercise in memory. With Frank it was pure nostalgia, their private time, because he wore the jacket only on festive occasions. If he knew what she was up to, he never let on.

He'd be impatient at first, then he'd get into the spirit. He'd close his eyes to remember.

"I wore it for David and Jenny's wedding. That was the year I twisted my ankle playing with the kids' pogo ball." (He'd open his eyes here.) "The ankle was almost healed, but I was worried I wasn't going to be able to dance on it. Remember, Elizabeth?"

She always said no, so he'd go on.

"You must remember. It was in the summer and we had the reception here. I had to scrub the patio three times to get rid of those darn mulberries and the bird dirt." (He hated that mulberry tree for attracting so many birds. She laughed, thinking about him cutting it down after the wedding. But the suckers from the roots came up every spring for three years. He mowed them down with the lawn mower, muttering the whole time. Finally he poured poison on them. It worked, but grass didn't grow there for two more years. He extended the patio to cover the dead spot so he could forget about the whole thing. She'd loved that tree, and the cedar waxwings, cardinals and grosbeaks it attracted. She was glad it had caused him a little grief.)

"The young people stayed until three a.m. and we were worried about the neighbours. I told David, if he was going to have it outdoors he'd better invite them all, but he never listened to me. Not once in his life. Oh well. We danced too. I remember. After everyone left we got out some old records—Tommy Dorsey—and we danced cheek-to-cheek. You were ripe that night, Elizabeth."

Often as he spoke, when the memories were good ones, she could feel their bodies get soft and full. Expanding out to meet each other. One time when Frank was telling mustard jacket memories—they were getting ready for David and Jenny's baby's christening—they went to bed! That was the first time they'd made love during the day since their honeymoon.

They never did find the jacket that day, and they were almost late for the christening, but they didn't mind. The poor baby cried through the whole ceremony and they didn't mind that either.

Elizabeth sits again. She holds the jacket in her arms the way she would a baby: head resting on the left arm, her right hand free. The hanger makes the shoulders feel as if there is substance inside and she aches to touch Frank's skin. It's been months since she and Frank have slept in the same bed.

She stands, slowly, and walks from the spare room to their bedroom. She hangs the jacket from the hook at the top of the full-length mirror. She runs her hands, thumbs outside the fabric, fingers inside, along the lapels, downwards to the waist button. She undoes it, dips her hands inside.

The lining is cool and smooth. She runs her hands upward toward the shoulders. She wants muscle and warmth. But when she reaches the wooden hanger she remembers how thin Frank is. From the cancer, the surgery, the unsuccessful chemo. How his collarbones stick out. How when he was weak and ill from the surgery, food dribbled down his whiskered chin and pooled in the hollow flesh between his neck and those collarbones. And how much she hated it when food got caught in his whiskers. She felt like screaming, "Don't let food stick there like that!" How he sensed her anger and looked at her, pleaded to know what was wrong, but she didn't tell him. She just washed him up, rubbed too hard, she supposed. God she hates food in whiskers!

Elizabeth takes the jacket off the hanger, lies down on the bed with it in her arms and cries. Frank is coming home today. She realizes if she doesn't cry now, she might not get another chance. Once Frank's home, she'll have to hold back and be cheerful. She reaches into the jacket pocket where she knows she'll find a folded white handkerchief. Some things never change. She always could count on Frank's handkerchiefs.

When she's cried out, she gets up and goes to the dresser. Frank will need a fresh handkerchief, his keys, and his package of du Maurier cigarettes. When Frank quit ten years ago, he still carried a fresh pack of cigarettes in the left-hand inside pocket of his jacket. Some people, once they gave up, got self-righteous, but not Frank. He loved to smoke, said he loved the smell of a match, that first taste of the tobacco, the feel of the smoke going in, then slowly coming out past his lips into the air. It was the most satisfying thing he'd ever done, he maintained, and he'd always have a cigarette ready for anybody who wanted one. Elizabeth can see him now, patting his lower right pocket for his keys and his left breast pocket for his cigarettes. It was his ritual. The last thing he did before they left to go anywhere.

Elizabeth covers the jacket with a drycleaner bag and hangs it in the back of the car. "Frank is coming home today," she says out loud as she drives. "Frank is coming home."

Frank is dressed in street clothes. He sits in a green vinyl chair by the window. One of those chairs that only hospitals seem to have these days. Seeing him in it makes Elizabeth's jaw tighten. When he turns to acknowledge her, she is lifting the bag from the jacket. He watches. A lightness uncreases his thin, clean-shaven face and Elizabeth thinks she feels him expanding toward her.

"My mustard jacket," he says. "Elizabeth."

There is quiet for ten heartbeats. Elizabeth counts every one of them in her chest. Frank stands and comes to her. She holds the jacket out and he slips his arms into the sleeves. She lets go; he adjusts the shoulders, does up the button. Elizabeth gathers his suitcase and a small plastic bag of laundry, and checks the bathroom. When she turns, she sees him pat his right pocket. The keys jingle. He pats his left for the cigarettes.

"Elizabeth," he says again. He holds his right arm out to her. She takes it and they leave the room together.

ROLLING

Frank and Elizabeth bought their burial plot, the one next to Robert, right after Robert died. They didn't want him to be alone. His wife was too young to commit herself to being buried near him, so they would do it. Why not? It was time for them to think of these things. Besides, look who else was here, they said, as we walked through the cemetery after visiting Robert's grave: Dr. Thomas, the orthopedic surgeon and the father of one of Robert's best friends was two rows over and several plots down.

And our neighbour's son, Bobby Zinken, had a stone nearby with his mother's name already on it, just waiting for her date of death to be added. Now wasn't that a coincidence; neighbours in life, neighbours in death. Remember Bobby's terrible car accident, they asked? And over by the hill was Ken Ferguson who'd been in the Knights of Columbus with my father, and whose family was even bigger than ours, almost two children to each one of us. Most of us had a Ferguson for a friend or classmate. Mine was Barry, who liked to talk and never asked me out, so we always stayed friends, even now.

Frank maintained that he would die first, that his body would go into the grave on the bottom and Elizabeth would come in on top of him. (A layer of cement would be poured between the caskets, the brochure told us, and the first casket must be lined with steel so the ground would not sag between burials.) Now there's a reversal, my father said, Elizabeth on top, and he laughed because he wanted us to know that he still thought about sex at his age, even here in a cemetery, and that he could joke in the face of death.

~

My father made it through the winter at home. When he got to the point where he needed to have fluid drained from his abdomen regularly, and he broke a rib because he coughed so hard, he had to go back into the hospital. My mother was afraid, she told me, that she would hurt my father, that the oxygen he sometimes needed would blow up; she was afraid that he would die.

It was spring. Crocuses had withered. Tulips were erect, long-stemmed, and shockingly garish, flagrantly unfurled. Lilac tips bulged, the purple of fresh bruises. Birds were cacophonous and tense, gaudy in their mating feathers.

In the hospital, my father didn't notice. On good days he gave orders: get me a tomato sandwich, or switch the channel to a police show—any one, it didn't matter, he preferred them now to nature shows which he said were filled with carnage and sex.

One day he told us he wanted "I Bid You Goodnight" and some good Catholic hymns sung at his funeral. He was groggy with drugs. He lay on his side, his eyes unfocussed but looking toward the window. He closed his eyes and we thought he was asleep. But he opened them again and asked if we'd set the date for the funeral yet. We looked at each other to see if we'd heard properly. "Dad," I told him, "you're in charge of that."

~

Some days, instead of visiting my father in the hospital, I visited my mother at the house where we grew up. From the outside nothing had changed. My father's fishing buddies, Vern Snyder and Cliff Gibson, kept my father's lawn as perfect as he would have kept it himself, raked, edged, waiting for the right combination of rain and sun to put fertilizer down. The rectangular corner beds were turned and ready for petunias. Vern said it was the least he could do, especially since he had a phobia about hospitals. The smells, he said.

Inside the house was another story. The television was off. My father was the first person on the block to buy a television. It was square and heavy, a glistening black screen in a cherry wood box. A point of light radiated outwards as it brought the screen to life. The same point glowed after the television was turned off.

My father learned about tubes and wires; he learned about aerial towers, ours scaling the side of the house and rising well above most others. We were the first to order in cable, but my father never did go for a satellite dish. He said that cable companies would fight for more channels and he was right.

My father was in the habit of turning on the TV the minute he woke up. He left it on until he fell asleep at night and my mother finally turned it off. As he went about his day he talked to the TV set, commented on the commentators, argued with news readers, yelled throughout sports matches. When he was younger it was Johnny Carson who lulled him to sleep, as he became more ill, it was more likely Peter Mansbridge reading the ten o'clock news.

He called us to watch this or that tidbit of a nature show or an exposé, excited by what he was watching, expecting us to share his enthusiasm. He recorded his favourite programs or specials so we would all have a chance to see them. His reference points were popular broadcasts: *Oprah, The Fifth Estate, Sixty Minutes,* Saturday sports, *Hockey Night in Canada*, the evening news.

"On *Oprah*," he'd declare, then tell us about anorexics, or daughters whose mothers were dating their boyfriends, or the improved lives of people who had had cosmetic surgery. Television provided the background to all family activities—meals, fights, games, chores, parties. "Turn the TV off," someone would shout when the noise became too much, but it never happened. One winter Max and I stayed with my parents in Florida where they had rented a trailer near Clearwater for a month. My father and I were the first to get up every morning. He turned the TV on, then went out to the screened porch to have his coffee. I turned it off. He immediately came in and turned it back on. He went out and I turned it off.

We did this for the two weeks of my stay, never once saying a word to each other about what we were doing. On. Off. On. I vowed never to take another holiday with my father, not on his turf at least. Max called us both children, said *he'd* never go on a holiday with either of us again so it was a moot point. I told him he just didn't understand. He rolled his eyes and walked out of the room.

My mother never cared for television. Though she kept my father company in the evening while he watched, she would knit or crotchet, and had even learned how to read, blocking out the TV blare. With my father in hospital the television was never turned on. I didn't really miss it, but the quiet was a constant reminder that my father had already gone from this house.

~

My father died on a Tuesday. My mother and David were with him. I told David I was sorry I wasn't there too. He told me that our father had a hard time getting a breath; David and my mother got to the point where they thought minutes were passing between each one. Then our father sat straight up in bed; where he got the strength David didn't know. "Oh no," our father said, then slumped back down, and was dead.

We decided on two days of visitation before the mass and burial. The funeral home, the same one where Robert had lain, was too hot, the thermostat set for winter temperatures. The flowers reeked. There were boxes of tissues on every table. My father looked too made up, too plumped up in the cheeks. His wedding band was far too big for his cancer-thinned fingers.

I thought of Robert's hands crossed so quietly on his body in his coffin. I remembered thinking how they should have been perfect, that the blemishes and spots should have been covered with cosmetics, or gone.

But Robert's hands were bigger than life. His fingernails were cracked along the edges and there were hints of dirt along his cuticles and in the cracks on his nails. On his fingerprints there were also faint swirls of dirt or grease as though he had just finished working on something mechanical, and washed, but traces remained.

I remembered how his hands were massive, out of proportion to his fine-boned wrists, and how they caressed the air when he talked. How he slipped the wedding band onto the finger of his new wife, while I worried that the band wouldn't fit. It did, guided carefully and slowly. How I was proud of him for doing this. When I saw his hands in the coffin, I couldn't believe they belonged to my brother, at the same time I knew with a fierce and hard loving that they did.

And I thought about my father's hands when he was younger. They were full of calluses, huge and hard. They were freckled across the back and covered with fine red-gold hairs that picked up the sun and shone like threads of copper. He let me trace the whorls on his hardened fingertips and press my fingernails into the toughness. He never flinched. I caressed his hands and his rough skin caught on the softness of my child hands, the way a broken fingernail catches on silk. His fingernails were nicked, had white spots and angry looking black marks on them.

I measured my growth against my father's hands: "Daddy, hold up your hand so I can see how big mine is." His hand was always bigger than mine, and thicker, more full of living. I was in awe of its size and power and strength.

I touched my father's bony hands in his casket. I worried his wedding band gently back and forth on his finger. His knuckle was still too big to have removed the ring.

My father was buried in the plot beside Robert. We threw roses into the grave with him. The smells were not of roses, but of the lilacs and apple blossoms that smothered the bushes and trees that grew throughout the cemetery in scandalous profusion.

We moved as a unit to the rolling hill. My mother took my hand and squeezed it. "Let's get it over with," she said.

We lay down, head to head, on the greening earth, and rolled. The ground was giving and warm. I heard voices and my sister's baby crying. And somewhere near my head, somersaulting round and round with me, I heard a sigh, then laughter.

Susan Zettell was born and raised in Kitchener, Ontario. She has also lived in Cambridge (Galt), Vancouver, Cape Breton and Halifax and now resides in Ottawa She began her studies at Carleton University, graduating from Dalhousie University in 1986. Her stories have been published in *The Capilano Review, The University of Windsor Review, The Canadian Forum* and *The New Quarterly*. Zettell has won first prize in the Nepean Library Short Story Contest and been a finalist in the CBC Literary Contest.

PRINTED AND BOUND
IN BOUCHERVILLE, QUÉBEC, CANADA
BY MARC VEILLEUX IMPRIMEUR INC.
IN OCTOBER, 1998